SATAN'S GUARDIANS MC

Book One — BRAND

Re-Edited/Formatted January 2022

COPYRIGHT © 2021 J.E. DAELMAN

All rights reserved

This book is a work of fiction. Names, characters, and events are the product of the author's imagination or have been used fictitiously. Do not construe them as real. Any resemblance to actual events or persons, living or dead, is purely coincidental.

This book or any portion thereof may not be reproduced or used in any manner whatsoever without the express written permission of the author. You cannot give for free on any kind of internet site.

This book is for readers over the age of 18 years. If bad language, violence, sexual encounters offend you, please do not read.

There may be mention of physical violence, torture, or abuse, but the series is a lighter version of MC. Hence, for example, rape *will never* be described in the series but may be mentioned.

Cover Designer: Oasis Book Covers
Editor: Richard Tonge
Alpha Reader: Marie D Vayer [USA]
Beta Readers: Karen Perez [USA] Sue Simanska [USA] Victor Saunders [UK] Emma Frost [UK]

NOTE

Please note, this author lives in the United Kingdom and has American Alpha and Beta readers who correct errors, but, as in other countries, it depends on which state you live as to how your slang or terms differ.

Therefore, although some words/terms you may think are incorrect are correct in one or more states.

REGISTERED

IF YOU HAVE NOT PURCHASED THIS COPY YOU NEED TO DELETE THE FILE AS IT IS STOLEN. PLEASE RESPECT THE AUTHORS RIGHT TO EARN AN HONEST LIVING.

You can read for free on Amazon with Kindle Unlimited

DEDICATION

This is for Richard, who owns my heart, picks me up when I am down, supports me no matter what I choose to do. I cannot imagine my life without him.
I love you, sweetie ♥

TABLE OF CONTENTS

COPYRIGHT © 2021 J.E. DAELMAN

Note

Registered

DEDICATION

TABLE OF CONTENTS

Chapter 1

Chapter 2

Chapter 3

Chapter 4

Chapter 5

Chapter 6

Chapter 7

Chapter 8

Chapter 9

Chapter 10

Chapter 11

Chapter 12

Chapter 13

Chapter 14

Chapter 15

Chapter 16

Chapter 17

Chapter 18

Chapter 19

Chapter 20

Chapter 21

Chapter 22

Chapter 23

Chapter 24

Books by J.E Daelman

ACKNOWLEDGEMENTS

You can find me here

CHAPTER 1

Driving up to the abandoned gas station Pip parked the SUV and sat looking at the property she had purchased. A truck stop is what they used to call it, now it's just a derelict building, but Pip has this image in her head that cannot be denied. She's going to make this work.

After losing her parents in a car accident nine months ago, Pip sold everything, and with her lawyer Larry Thomas's help, she placed all her eggs in one basket and moved to make a fresh start. Leaving Stanhope, Nebraska relocating to Cougar Creek, Montana. She now has $7 million sitting in her account after purchasing this pile of bricks, money won't bring her parents back, but it will give her a step forward.

Pip has to get organized and get workers out here to do what she needs to make her dream come true. A new trailer is being delivered on-site today. Looking at her watch, she had made good time and is here well before the driver arrives.

Parking, she opens her vehicle door and hops out, turning to call her all-black German Shepherd 'Coal.' He is a 2-year-old rescue she fell in love with at first sight. On this new venture in life, she didn't want to start on her own. She had visited the rescue center for something she could call family and hoped to feel less lonely. He is massive, always alert but gentle with her as if he knows her soul needs to heal. Pip is 5' 6", auburn hair down past her shoulders, curvy figure, but not an ounce of fat after all the stress these last few months; Coal reaches just under waist height.

Walking around the lot, she sees the perfect spot for the trailer, not too close that any building work will be damaging but not too far that once she opens, it will be in easy reach, she can pop back for Coal anytime she likes, and she can see a water source available, perfect.

Pip takes a deep breath and releases it slowly, puts her hand out to tickle Coal behind his ears, and then looks down at him with a smile on her face. Life begins again now runs through Pip's mind.

'Ok, let's start living,' she says to Coal and, with that, takes her first steps toward the building and opens the door.

Stepping into the dismal property, Pip sees the old, broken tables, chairs, and side booths, the counter that at some time would have been the hub of the room, behind that the open hatch where you can see into the kitchen area.

Everything in this building is going to be stripped out and replaced with modern equipment. She will need to find suitable kitchen hands, and she won't be hiring anyone who can't show they have anything but the achievement of this place in mind.

The excitement starts to rumble through her system as she steps into the kitchen area. Oh boy, this is such a darn mess, a good thing it will all be going, as looking at it, nothing would be worth saving. Stepping to the back door, Pip checks the other two keys she was given and tries the one she thinks may fit, and opens it to let the fresh air filter in. She finds a piece of wood that has broken from the frame and jams it under the door to keep it open.

Looking to the back of the property, she views the 37 acres of beautiful land behind this plot which she purchased, no idea what will happen with it, but it's too stunning to let a damn construction company get their hands on. If nothing is ever done with it, it means they can't build a nasty housing estate either.

A crunching of tires from the front of the plot can be heard. Pip rushes back through the building and out the door to see the trailer is being delivered. She calls to the driver and points in the direction to where she wants it to be set up, a good thing this place has a massive parking area at the back for him to turn around.

The driver stops, he and his passenger jumped out to walk over to Pip, and between them, they decide exactly where to place the trailer and set it up. She is relieved she paid extra to have the set-up of the gas, generator, and thankfully water too.

Leaving the driver and his partner to do what they have to; she calls Coal and jogs back to her vehicle. She can get her boy out the way, so no accidents happen. Opening the door, she tells Coal to jump into the back seat. Making sure she has the windows wide for him, she grabs his bowl and fills it with cold water from one of the thermoses she has. Pip opens a second thermos so she can have a drink of coffee herself.

Leaning on her SUV while sipping her coffee, her mind wanders to how her parent's accident happened, still feeling that it was not an accident at all but having no way of proving otherwise. They were both lawyers and were partners in a practice that was highly thought of, but they had been a little secretive the few weeks before they died. They were not their usual selves. They were always serious about and around their work, but when they got home to Pip, they were chatting and happy to be with each other and her.

That was not the case those last few weeks. They kept giving each other looks, jumpy when the phone rang and double-checking, they had locked the door. Pip had asked what was the matter, what they were worried about, but they kept saying all was fine.

After the funeral, Pip had spoken to their business partner in the practice and asked if anything had been happening at work to have her parents jumpy, and he said he had no idea, but he looked shifty and wouldn't make eye contact. Something was not right for sure.

Stephen Woolcombe was known to be a ruthless lawyer, but Pip had never had to have dealings with him, and as her parents had used a different company to make their will, that again made her think something could be wrong because why go somewhere else when you owned the top firm in town! In fact, the best firm in three states.

Stephen Woolcombe surprised her when he asked if he could buy her out of the company. At that time, it was less than a month since her parents died and two weeks since burying them. In the will, they advised that she keep her 50% share of the partnership as a silent partner, but once a year, she has an independent auditor in to make sure all was running as it should.

When she refused to sell her share of the partnership, Stephen was not happy and tried to push her. Still, Pip stood firm and told him straight she would not sell. She would not interfere in the running of the company either. Every year at this time, she would have an independent check done on the company, which was all above board and highly recommended by her lawyer. She also told him that she wanted her income from the business paid into an account annually rather than monthly.

Pip still had an uneasy feeling about Stephen, her parent's death, and why things kept going wrong around her. First, her parent's house had been vandalized. Then her car was torched while she was at her bank sorting all her finances and lastly, her father's secretary June had slipped her a note when she was leaving

Stephen's office which told her to be careful, watch her back and get the hell out of Dodge fast!

Pip sold everything apart from some of her clothes, photo albums, and jewelry her mother owned. She didn't need anything to drag her down as her parents wouldn't want her to be held back with things that could be replaced, her memories will never go, and that is what was most important to her.

CHAPTER 2

The driver startled her out of her thoughts, calling Pip to come and check out the trailer and show her how to use everything now it is all set up and working. Walking toward him out of the corner of her eye, she sees a cop cruiser slowly driving past. Thinking nothing of it, Pip steps up her pace and smiles at the driver. "Yep, let's get done so you can get off."

The driver also noted the cruiser and, once at the trailer, looked Pip in the eye and said, "That cop may come across as nice, but lady, he's not. You need to be careful where he's concerned. This is a friendly warning as you're new here. Now let me show you how I have you set up." The driver goes through opening and closing the gas connectors and the generator settings.

Once Pip was happy with everything, the driver takes off for his next job of the day, and she brings her SUV over near to the trailer and parks it at the side. Opening the door, she lets Coal jump out, and she starts the task of taking boxes into the trailer and putting everything away, feeling optimistic about the future.

Ninety minutes later, she is hot and flagging, needing a drink and something to eat. As she decided to do that, Coal starts to growl, which has Pip's hair standing on end as it is deep, and he means it. She opens her purse and pulls out her Glock 9 mm her father gave her for her 18th birthday and subsequently taught her how to clean and use it. She has a concealed carry permit and has no problem using it if she has to.

Pip stealthily walks to the door of the trailer and slides her hand into Coal's flat collar as she doesn't want him dashing out before her. Slowly she moves out the door and, holding her gun in one hand and Coal in the other, she noted immediately the officer that had more than likely been patrolling past earlier. She didn't move. She waited for what came next. She wasn't going to say anything as she kept her eye on him to see what he would do.

****PIP****

Officer Bruce Tailor is about 6' I guess, a bit overweight, and for an officer of the law, he is pretty shabby. He cocks his head to the side and looks me over, from my head to my feet and back again, giving me a sleazy grin.

"Well, hello, little lady, what's going on here?" he asks, stepping closer, to which Coal takes a dislike and growls harder.

"Good day Officer, I purchased the property and the land behind, so I am moving into my trailer while I get it all renovated as I will be reopening." but that is all I am willing to provide. I don't want to give him my name or anything at this stage if I can help it.

"Is there a problem?" I ask as he keeps looking at me without responding.

He tries again to take a step forward, and Coal growls louder and longer this time. "Can you put your dog into the trailer so we can speak?" he asks while giving Coal a worried look.

"Nope, I can't, he stays by my side, I have his collar, he's not stepping towards you at all, and if you state what you want to talk to me about, we can get done, and I can get on with my day."

I recognize that he is not happy with my response, but I don't give a damn what he likes. I'm breaking no laws and have no problem with standing my ground. Unbeknownst to him, the video cam in my vehicle is still recording. This camera was a purchase I made on a recommendation from my lawyer when he knew my plans and that I would be on my own. It has a built-in solar panel to keep it charged. It can record when the vehicle is switched off. Hence the Officer is being recorded as we speak.

The Officer gives me another sick grin and removes his hat, then runs his hand over his short greasy hair. Yuck is my first impression.

"Well, little lady, how about I take you out for a touch of dinner tonight, and we can get to know each other, you know, real friendly-like," he says, licking his lips.

"Oh, I'm sorry, at this time, I am not dating, eating out, or anything else as I have far too much to do." and my response was pretty cool as I felt like being sick all over him.

I could see he was going to come back with a nasty retort with the setting of his face, but as he opens his mouth, we both look to the front of the property as five bikes rolled to a stop, bringing with them plenty of noise, revving of engines and dust. I felt like I should whoop with joy as it put a total stop to this conversation.

He steps back and starts to wander toward his vehicle without another word in my direction. He is glaring at the bikers. Although they have not spoken to him, they are giving him nasty looks back. My stomach starts to knot as I hope nothing is going to kick off here. Coal growls once more, and glancing down at him, I see he's focused on the Officer and not the bikers, which surprised me, to say the least, but I keep holding his collar, and I still have my hand tight on my Glock, which is against my right thigh ready to use if needed.

Officer Tailor gets in his cruiser and takes off, leaving bits of gravel from the broken parking area kicking up under his wheels. Once he is out onto the road, I suck in a deep breath, slowly pushing it out, and then look toward the bikers.

The lead biker turns off his engine, the others follow suit, and he takes off his helmet, placing it onto his bike seat. Gee, he is over six feet of real man meat is my first thought, panty wetting material for sure, brown hair with flecks of blond through it due to the sun, well-built too from what I can see.

I stand there looking and waiting, Coal has calmed down and is now sitting at my side, which takes me by surprise as he is relaxed, go figure, one cop, and he is on alert, five bikers, and he wants a nap!

'Mr. man meat' saunters over with this swagger while his buddies get off their bikes and stand around watching, but I note the one at the back is still keeping an eye on the road, in the direction the cruiser went.

"My name is Brand or Pres. I'm President of the Satan's Guardians MC. We reside up the road in the compound that you can see from the road. We just wanted to drop in to say welcome and ask if you needed anything at all?"

I stand there staring at him like he has two heads when I notice he starts to smirk with one side of his mouth, making a dimple pop out. I suddenly realize I am looking like an idiot and quickly shove my hand out to shake his, but I had forgotten I still have my Glock in it, five guns are pointing straight at me, Coal jumps up and growls, showing all his teeth and every hair on his body must be standing on end.

"Oh shit, I'm sorry, I forgot I had it in my hand," and I put the Glock quickly in the waistband of my jeans against my spine. Again, I slowly hold my hand out and say, "Hi, thank you for the welcome, and my name is Piper, but everyone calls me Pip."

He nods over his shoulder to the others, and they stand down. He takes my hand and shakes it, and hangs on to it for a bit longer than I thought he should.

"I'm thankful you showed up when you did as Officer Sleaze was creeping me out a bit, to be honest," I say and blush as I blurted that out there for all to hear. Gosh, I must have spent too much time on my own as I seem to have lost the skill of conversing correctly.

"Glad we could help," he responds with this deep rumbling voice that makes me want to melt against him, "Be careful of that Officer, he is not all he seems, but I'm sure you'll make up your own mind given time. Have you purchased this old property?" He asks while scanning the area with what, I notice, are gorgeous chocolate-colored eyes.

"Yes, I'm going to renovate it and reopen. I'm going to be looking for workers of all types and then staff, of course, once I'm near completion. Can you recommend anyone? I'm new around here and know no one as yet." I hope he has some knowledge of decent workmen, as I do need a nudge in the right direction.

"Satan's Guardians MC owns a construction company if you're interested. We have a good reputation for the work we do. You can check out the reviews on our website. We also own a garage further down the road, so if you ever need repairs, it's not far away," as he finishes saying this, he takes out his cell phone and tells me to give him my number then he can text his contact details.

I let go of Coal's collar and step into the trailer, grab my cell phone and go back out while switching it on as I have no one to contact at this time. I left my friend 'Liza' behind as she didn't want to leave her catering job, her contract has another ten months to run.

We exchange numbers, and I ask if he would like to look in the building, then he will have an idea of how much work will need to be done. He shouts out to one of the men, and they both walk at my side to the front of the property. Coal trots alongside with his tongue lolling out.

Brand introduces me to Shades, who happens to be the boss of the construction business. Shades must be 6' 4" black hair and all muscle. He takes a notepad out of his back pocket and a pencil which is so small it is a wonder it has any lead left in it. I think he must be called Shades as he has not taken his sun shades off.

"Yep, that's why they call me Shades," he says all that with a grin on his face, and it's now apparent I had spoken aloud when I had thought I'd said it in my head, I couldn't help it and for the first time in a long while I laughed.

The three of us go into the building, and I start giving them the lowdown of what I have in my mind's eye. We will have to strip it down to the brick, re-wire, re-plaster, and build it all back with everything new.

"Do you realize how much this is going to cost you?" Brand states with an eyebrow lift.

"Well, of course, I have a vague idea. I have a million-dollar budget for this part here. Will that not be enough?" I respond with a touch of sass, I must admit. Brand looks at Shades, who then lifts his eyebrow at me, but I cannot tell what he is thinking as he still has his damn shades on.

"If it will cost more, it's not an issue. I have more," I state and feel like stamping my foot.

"We need to rip everything out, have it hauled away, then rebuild from the ground up. Will you want just the building done, or will you want us to do the parking area too?" Shades inquires.

"Well, I want the lot done too, but I don't want different people to do different things. I just want to go through what is needed, then let you get on with it," I reply. "Oh, I will want the upstairs remodeled, so the apartment up there is livable. Once this is all done, I will want a house built out back somewhere as I own all that property. Will that be too much for you, or can you do it all?" I ask, hoping they can do it because I don't want more than one company working here.

Again, Brand and Shades look at each other and then turn back to me.

"We can do all that, but you know we are talking probably working for a year or more to get all that done? Are you okay with that timeline, and depending on how large you want the house, we are talking between 1.5 and 2 million, I would think with all the appliances, the supplies, and wages, etc.?" Shades states.

"Yes, to all that Shades, now how much would you need upfront to make a start? And would you want a monthly payment, a lump sum, how do you want to do this? Also, I'll need someone to go with me to look at appliances, etc., as I don't know this area at all. Would that be viable?" I am trying to put it all out in the open and giving my trust, which I hope will not come back and bite me later.

Brand steps forward now, "I think a three-month down payment for getting started so we can pay wages, you pay for supplies and appliances as we go along, then at three monthly intervals we give you an invoice for work done, how does that sound to you?"

"Perfect, give me an invoice ASAP, and we can get started," I respond, and with that, I spit on my hand, I hold it out as the deal is done, they both laugh, spit and shake, I don't think my smile can be wider.

CHAPTER 3

****PIP****

The next few days are busy with the interior of the building being ripped out and carted away. Walking through the property now, it all looks more extensive, with nothing but walls, pipes showing, and broken plaster. The upstairs apartment is all ripped out. The canvas is how I see it, to a whole new adventure and one I hope will give me purpose and a feeling of achievement.

I am thankful my parents insisted I do something with a career in mind and receiving my chef diploma was something I had wanted since being a child and making my first cakes with my mother.

I look at the brochures in my hand and search around for Shades. I want to know if he'll have time in the next couple of weeks to go with me or tell me where to look and order everything we'll need. I could purchase online if I have to, but I would enjoy seeing it before I buy.

I find Shades behind the building with a redhead rubbing her hands all over him, ass hanging out of her shorts, top hardly covering her chest and stripper heels. I mean, it isn't even lunchtime yet, puleeeeezzee.

I glance at my watch, nip back into the building, and see Cali busy in the kitchen area, taking plaster off the walls. He's an incredible sight to see, 6' 2", blonde, man bun, well-muscled, and he's always smiling.

"Cali," I shout as I continue walking in, hoping to get his attention.

"Yeah, what's up, Pip?" he replies, looking towards me.

"Do you want a drink? I'm going to nip into town and grab us all some lunch. Do you want something drink-wise while I'm there?" I ask.

After he wipes his forehead and steps a bit nearer smiling, he says, "I'll have whatever you bring Pip, I'm easy-going drink-wise. Coffee or a cold one is fine by me."

"Ok, shall I just bring for Whisky, Ice, and Gunner too?"

"Yeah, that's cool, Pip." he moves back to breaking up plaster.

I decided to check with Whisky, Ice, and Gunner for drinks, then take off to see what Shades wants. He's still talking to the redhead, and she's all over him.

"Shades, you want a drink with your lunch?" I shout to him.

He glances my way, and when he sees me, he looks a bit embarrassed but shouts to me, "Na, I'm ok, thanks, Pip." the redhead gives me a nasty glare, and I throw one right back to her.

"Who the fuck is she?" asks the redhead to Shades.

"Shut the fuck up, Babs," he shouts.

I wouldn't say I like this at all, my business property, my time, I'm paying for all this, I glance at my watch, and it is twenty-five minutes since I last looked. I do what my gut tells me to do.

"Get off my property now," I tell this bitch.

She grins and says, "Make me."

"Ok," I reply and take my gun from my back waistband and point it straight at her. "Move off my property, NOW."

Shades moves in front of this redhead and drags her around the corner of the building. I follow them both, keeping my gun pointed, and at the ready, they are bickering, but I can't hear what they are saying. Shades pushes her into a rusty old banger, and she takes off after she gives me another nasty look and a middle finger.

I put my gun away and turn to move back towards my trailer as I need to grab my purse. Shades catches up and starts to apologize, but I put my hand up.

"I don't want to hear it Shades, if you want to mix with skanks, that's up to you, but I don't want you to do it here or on my time, end of, I'm not discussing this with you, if this happens again, I'll speak to Brand about replacing you, or I find another company. I will not be disrespected on my property."

I don't wait for him to reply as I need this shit like a hole in the head. A half dozen steps, and I turn back toward him. He is still watching me walk away.

"But Shades, you ever need to redden my ear at all. You can do it any time after work!" with that, I leave him to it.

In my trailer, I drop the brochures and grab my purse.

"Come on, Coal, you can have a ride and get out of this place for a while," he wags his tail and stands at the door, ready.

While driving into town, I put on the radio and sing along to the current tune. I see through my rearview that a vehicle is coming up behind me pretty damn fast. My eyes flick between the mirror and the road ahead. Flashing lights appear, making me groan as our vehicles are the only ones at the moment on this stretch. Hence, he has to want me to pull over.

I glide onto the hard shoulder but leave my engine running as I see it is Officer Tailor. Winding my window down, I'm thankful I didn't put Coal in the back. If I need him, he is handy at least.

"What seems to be the problem, Officer?" I say sweetly, but I don't like the look on this asshole's face.

"You were speeding, at least 20 over the limit," he nastily spits.

Oh dear, I think our first meeting didn't go down well, and this is his form of payback.

Knowing I have to cover my ass, I open the passenger window wide and tell Coal to stay. Then I push out of my door, making Officer Shithead move back. I walk to the front of my SUV, where I know the cam will get all this conversation.

"I'm not sure what makes you think I was speeding, Officer Tailor." I respond again sweetly, "You tore up behind me from nowhere, then put your lights on. How would you think I was speeding when you were doing 50 over the limit?" I know I should not have been that bit sassy, but I couldn't stop myself.

"No matter if you were or not, I am citing you a ticket for speeding, and if I catch you again, I'll haul you in, and I **will** haul you in as I know the next time you're in your vehicle, you will be speeding," he responds with a nasty grin on his face.

"So, you're telling me I was not speeding, but you're ticketing me as you just feel like it, is that right? Oh, and you will ticket me again when I come off my property!" I'm getting angry at this point.

"Exactly," he replies with a self-satisfied look on his face.

"Ok, give me my ticket, and I will see you in court when I don't pay it," I respond, he is not happy about this, but I am past caring.

"This could all go away if you want to have dinner and a nice time afterward." the sleaze of the force states, to which I laugh, grab my ticket, and get back in my vehicle, driving off before anything else can be said.

Now I am fed up and angry, and although the day started well, it has sure gone downhill pretty quickly, and it isn't lunchtime yet.

I visit the grocery store, nip next door to purchase some cold beers, of which I get a mixture as I have no idea what anyone wants. I grab a bottle of southern comfort because it is my all-time favorite drink with lots of ice. It slides down nice and cool. I cannot wait now for bedtime and a tall glass. Then I go to the drive-in and grab a ton of food for everyone, as no way am I cooking in the trailer for that many.

Driving back, I note the patrol cruiser is following me again. I grab my cell phone and see who I can contact. Brand's number catches my eye. Well, I am short of anyone around here that I can name as a friend. I am low on options. I call his number, and after a couple of rings, he answers.

"Hi Pip, what's up?" he quickly says.

"Brand, I'm sorry to call you, but I had a run-in with Officer Tailor on my way into town, now I am on my way back to feed everyone lunch, and he showed up again behind me, oh shit, he is flashing his lights to pull me up again. I am about three minutes away from my property. What do I do?" I say as fast as I can. I can feel my heart starting to race as I don't know what this asshole will throw at me now.

"Stop and stay calm Pip, I'll be with you in two minutes." and he hangs up.

I take my time pulling up on the hard shoulder, making sure my passenger side window is open if Coal needs to get out in a hurry. He's rattled for sure. He's growling and fixated on Officer Tailor. I half-open my window but sit and wait.

Officer Shithead as I have now started to name him, in my mind, gets out of the patrol car and strolls up with a nasty grin on his face. I keep mine bland, no reaction at all. I won't give him the satisfaction.

"Get out of the vehicle." he spits at me.

I switch off my engine and undo my seatbelt, not rushing as I want the time to pass slowly, to give Brand a chance to get to me. I tell Coal to stay and open my door, climbing out.

"Hands-on, the hood, spread your legs." he snaps out.

"No," I respond. "You've not told me why you've pulled me over. What's your reason this time?" While I am saying this, I move as I need this to be on the cam. I want to get us in range once more. This has to be recorded too.

"I don't need a reason. I can do as I like, and you're going to spread 'um, get your hands on your hood." He again gives me that nasty grin.

Then I hear the bikes. Thank God, there was no way I was spreading my legs for this shithead. Four bikers come to a stop in front of us, and Brand looks straight at me and gives me a slight nod, then slides his leg over his seat and gets off the bike, Patch, Trigger, and Torch copy Brand's move to stand together.

"Now what have we got here?" Brand asks, stepping, so he is between myself and Officer Tailor.

I quickly step nearer him and say. 'This Officer pulled me over for no reason and demanded I put my hands on the hood and spread my legs, to which I refused."

Brand steps nearer Officer Shithead, and I turn slightly and whisper to Torch that my camera is working on the dash and is recording.

Hence, Brand has to be careful as I'll use this against Tailor in court if I need to.

Torch nods and moves behind his Pres and whispers in his ear, to which Brand looks at me and smirks.

"What are you pulling Pip over for Bruce?" Brand asks.

The response took my breath away.

"She is under arrest for possession of class A narcotics." he spits out.

"Where are these narcotics, Officer? You have not searched my vehicle or my property, so I want to know where these narcotics supposedly are?" I respond and start to vibrate with rage.

Thankfully I had kept my cell phone in my pocket. I take a look at it and ring my lawyer Larry while dodging Officer Shithead, who at this stage is trying to grab me or the phone, and if it weren't so serious, I would laugh as Patch, Trigger, and Torch keep themselves between myself and the Officer.

I promptly tell the lady that answers the phone I must speak to Larry Thomas, my lawyer, as I am on the side of the road with an officer trying to arrest me. She puts me straight through. I quickly fill Larry in on what a crock of bull this is and what is going on. Larry tells me to hand the phone to the Officer, which I do.

After a few minutes, Tailor gets red in the face with a temper, gives me back my cell phone and tells me I am lucky today, and takes off in his vehicle with his anger on full display.

I look at my phone, and Larry is still on the line. I ask what happened, and he fills me in on the conversation he had and that I need not be worried as he has it all under control. He has demanded all the evidence, if any, be sent to him within 48hrs and if none is forthcoming, then he will slam Officer Tailor for harassment. I inform Larry that I have the whole thing on my cam. I will forward it all to his office if he wants it.

Larry tells me to watch out for this officer. He was going to do some digging and that this false narcotics crap was nothing to worry about, and he'd sort it out and get back to me in a couple of days. He will reach out to Bill Forest, his old mate at the FBI, to see what he may or may not know or if he can find out anything about this Tailor character.

Turning to Brand, I repeat what Larry told me, and he puts his arm around my shoulders and kisses me on my forehead, taking me by surprise.

"Don't worry, Pip, keep your head down a few days. If you need anything fetching, ring Billy 'The Kid', the club's newest prospect." Brand advises me.

"I don't understand why he is targeting me with all this bullshit? I'm pleased we have this on the camera," I replied, shaking my head and move toward my vehicle.

"I just want to thank you all for coming to help me. I have to admit I was scared when he told me to spread um." they all growl at this and stand with their fists clenched.

"We'll follow you back, Pip," said Brand. We take off, and I have to say I am happy none of us were arrested.

CHAPTER 4

####*PIP****

Three days later, Larry rings and informs me it's all cleared up as the officer had no evidence of anything at all. It was all false bullshit. His friend in the FBI was going to look into the officer as obviously something was not right with him.

The weekend came around, and no men are working. It's quiet and a bit eerie being on my own. I grab my gun target and walk to the back of the parking area, and set up. I make sure Coal is in the trailer safely out of the way, and then I clear my mind and do a session with my Glock, 15 rounds a time, I must have used 100+ rounds, but I do feel better for it. Back in the trailer, I clean my gun and then myself.

"Come on, Coal, let's go for a walk," we go out into the back property, acres of it, and we walk where and when we can for over an hour. I am pleased I grabbed my backpack with the bowl, water, and a flask as I find us somewhere to sit and enjoy a breather. We then trudge all the way home again, enjoying the peace on the way.

When we arrive back, I am surprised to see Billy 'The Kid' prospect sitting on my trailer steps.

"Hi, Billy, how are you doing? What can I do for you?" I say while I am still a bit breathless.

"Hi Pip, I came over to see if you need anything brought back from town as I'm going in to get some bits for the clubhouse," he stands from the step and rubs his hand behind Coal's ears.

"Oh, no thanks, Billy. I have everything for the moment. Can I ask you for a bit of advice?" I say, with hopes he will have some reliable information he can give me.

"Of course, if I can help, I sure will," Billy replies looking at me curiously.

"Ok, I am a bit worried about being on my own after the trouble with Officer Tailor, and I was going to look for a security company to put up some fencing and cameras but not sure where to go. Do you have any ideas?" I ask, dropping my backpack inside the trailer door.

"Well, Pip, it just so happens you can contact Spider or Ace at our "BeSecure" Security Company. Let me grab a card out of the van for you," he says. Billy hands me the business card." They are really good and have an excellent reputation." he pats me on the shoulder and takes off for town.

No time like the present, I suppose, I ring the first number on the card, which happens to be Spider.

On answering, I quickly say, "Hi, this is Pip. SGMC is doing construction for me."

Before I can say more, "Hi Pip, this is Spider. How can I help you?"

"Well, Spider, I need your security company to come out and put up some fencing and cameras for me as I don't feel very safe at the moment with that Officer Tailor being an asshole," I state. "It's a large property, so you will need to get some measurements, I would think."

Spider chuckles at my description and asks, "What about I come out tomorrow?" which is Sunday. "To have a look at the whole site."

"That suits me, Spider, as I'm not going anywhere tomorrow." and we make a time for early afternoon.

****

Tomorrow comes around reasonably quickly, and when Spider arrives on his Harley, I admire it with the skull and flames all blended in perfectly on the tank.

"That is pretty awesome, Spider. I love it," I blurt out, to which Spider smiles and tells me he has an artist friend who loves to play with tanks, and he is trying to get her to turn it into a viable business instead of a hobby.

"Does this friend do any kind of work? Like designing for flyers, business cards, anything business related? I am looking for someone to help me do some designs inside and outside once we have completed the other work," I state.

"I don't think she has, but I'll surely ask her. She's in a bit of a bad place at the moment financially, so this may be a good thing for her. I'll get back to you when I've spoken to her," Spider replies.

We spend over an hour walking the property boundary, going in and out of the building, then upstairs to the apartment. Spider evaluates all the security I'll need, which is not a small amount. Coal happily trots along beside us. I need to get the internet up and running as quickly as possible as I want it available in the trailer, the business, and the apartment.

We are standing outside now, and Spider is jotting down on his tablet all the equipment we'll need for the job, Coal suddenly starts to growl, and he turns to look at the back property staring intently.

He heard something. The hair on the back of my neck stands up, but I can't see anything.

Spider is scanning the area too, but he sees nothing.

"I think we'll add some cameras pointing to the back as well, Pip." Spider states, and I agree readily. With that, Coal calms and seems to be happy again, odd, but this is something else that has made me feel uneasy.

After this incident, the day is quiet and passes without any further problems. I clean the trailer, do some laundry and then shower. Making a drink, I grab the brochures and a notepad and start going through to select all the items that will be needed to rebuild the kitchen. I create a hefty list of stoves, fridges, mixers, blenders, and it goes on and on.

As night falls and the darkness starts to creep in, I get a real uneasy feeling. It grows as Coal becomes more alert. Something's not right. I check my Glock as I don't want to be caught out without it. I open the trailer door and let Coal out but tell him to stay. We both stand and remain alert, then Coal starts to growl facing the back property again, and he is looking into the area he was attentive to earlier in the day. I can't see anything, but that doesn't mean nothing is there.

After a few minutes, Coal calms once more, and the stillness of the night seems to ease him. Whatever was there, I am sure, has gone but was it, man or beast, I think to myself.

Settling back in the trailer, I lock the door, grab water and ring my friend Liza. When Liza answers, I'm relieved

"Hi Liza, how are you doing? I'm missing you."

"Oh Pip, it's so good to hear you. I'm good. Catering itself is going well, but I am thinking of leaving this company and going out on a limb on my own in the future. I'm sick of being pushed around by this asshole boss and having no credit for the work I do." Liza responds and is having a hard time but does not want to admit it.

After chatting for twenty minutes or so, I jump in with both feet and say, "Liza, why don't you come here to me? I'll have the business up and running, and I can build on an extra area for you, a catering business. It could have a food area, pantries, and an office we can share. You would be independent, and I am being selfish as I would have you here with me," I hold my breath for her reply.

"Oh my god, Pip, I miss you so much, and I would love to be there with you, but how would I pay you back for all that? It would take years to accumulate that sort of finance." Liza rushes to say.

"No, Liza, it would be part and parcel of this building, so if you insist, you could pay a small rent, after the first year anyway, but it would be your catering business, not mine, not part of my business. It would work. The two businesses would run side by side, hand in glove, so to speak. Could you give it some thought and let me know? Now I'm going to bed as I have a busy day tomorrow. Love you, girl," and we say goodnight and that we will talk soon.

I genuinely hope Liza will agree to come and be a part of my life once more. Losing my parents has been challenging but not having my friend as well, making it tougher still. She could live in the apartment above the building too, once completed, as I know she likes to be independent. Many thoughts are running through my head as I finally fall asleep.

CHAPTER 5

****PIP****

A*wake early*, and the morning is still quiet, I quickly get dressed, grab a drink, and let Coal out. I sit on the trailer steps while I wait for him to come back. I can see him as he seems to have picked a specific area to do his business, making it easy for me to clean up after him.

When he comes back, I grab his bowl and food and set him up with fresh water. While he's eating, I put on my shoulder holster, get my gun and take a walk to the area Coal was looking at yesterday. Searching around, I don't see anything out of place, but then scanning the ground, I can see footprints and a couple of cigarette butts. This confirms someone was watching. I return to the trailer and remove my gun and make sure Coal is safely inside.

Shades and his team turn up and quickly get busy, which I am thankful for as there is a lot of work to get through. I wander over and ask Shades if he would have time soon to look at the appliances I'll need or if he thinks I'll have to order online. He's happy to go with me later in the week, and we plan on Thursday if all goes well, which gives me three days to finish my list of things I'll need.

I want to speak to Spider today and make sure he knows what's happening. He can cover this area well or put fencing up to stop anyone from getting nearer. This is a worry now, and it confirms something about this place or myself is not right. No time like the present, I nip back to the trailer and grab my cell.

Four rings, and Spider answers, "Morning Spider, it's Pip. I want to update you before you purchase what you need. I had another incident last night. Coal was aware someone was around again on the back property, and this morning I checked it out, there were footprints and a couple of cigarette butts, so can you have a look and determine if it needs all fencing in?" I state, chewing my lip as I am a bit anxious.

"I'll come over in half an hour, Pip, and we can have a look and decide what we are going to do about it," he responds. I can hear people talking behind him. He must be at work.

Sure enough, half an hour later sees Spider arriving with none other than Brand alongside him. They are in a truck with "BeSecure" on the sides and some materials in the bed. They both jump out and stroll over to where I am standing at the side of the building.

"Morning Pip." Brand greets with that smile that makes his dimple pop.

"Hi Brand, how are you today?" I respond, and for some reason, I feel nervous talking to him. He is such a stunning-looking man. To be near him makes my heart race.

As he starts to respond, another truck pulls in, and a tall man with jet black hair, six-foot-plus, I would think, jumps out. He has a nasty scar on the left side of his face. It starts under his eye and runs halfway down his cheek. He ambles straight over to us, grabs my hand, and kisses my knuckles, to which I burst out laughing.

"Hi Pip, I'm Ace, and I'm fortunate to meet you," all said with a massive grin on his face and much to the annoyance of Brand, who is giving him a dirty look.

"Well, hello Ace, it is nice to meet you also." I cheekily respond but make sure I get my hand back at the same time.

Spider intervenes at this point, saying, "Fucks sake, Ace, get a grip. Anyone would think you've never seen a beautiful woman before.

Right Pip, the area that Coal was looking at yesterday, is that where you saw the footprints?"

"Yes, there was a couple of cigarette butts too. Do you want me to show you?" I start to walk in that direction as I am speaking.

"No, it's ok Pip, let Ace have a look. We can decide what we'll need to do about keeping you safe." Spider is again scanning the perimeter of the property as he is speaking to me.

"Pip, I know it's a large area, but I think we should fence you off all around the parking area. If you want, we can put a gate in at the bottom to get through to the other area at the back if you need to. If we use good fencing, it will be great to stay up once the business is open too." states Brand.

"I like that idea because I am starting to feel uneasy about being here alone. What with Officer Shithead and now this unknown person, it's leaving me a bit prickly." which I say while looking at the floor as I am embarrassed to admit it.

Ace saunters back and states, "The area has certainly had some activity in the last few days, you can tell by the fresh footprints, and the butts are still fairly fresh, so not many hours since they were dropped, whoever it was didn't even bother stepping them out either. Spider, you said Coal growled and reacted, so whoever this was is now aware that the dog has a good sense of the area. To keep Pip safe, we need to get the area fenced in, and we need the cameras up and running ASAP. In the meantime, Brand, do you think we could put 'Shoes' up here to watch at night?"

"Who is Shoes?" I ask. I feel pretty nervous about it all now, I have to admit, but I don't want to look like a baby when I'm going to be a businesswoman. I need to make sure I keep positive, and my gun stays at hand.

Brand replies, "Shoes is one of our prospects, been with us about six months now, reliable, polite too, he's a bit shy, he takes all his tasks we give out seriously, so he's a good choice to go on night duty."

"Alright, I'm happy with that if you are. I don't think it will hurt me to have some company around here after you guys leave. Could even put up the BBQ and have a meal with him in an evening," saying that makes me smile as it is nice to think of having a bit of company.

"Oh no, you don't feed him or make him comfortable. He needs to be on his toes," Brand spits out.

"Well, that won't work for me. I cannot sit and eat and not be social. I'm a chef, after all. My whole way of life revolves around feeding people good food, nope, if he is here, he will eat with me, and you won't be here to see it," I snap back at him.

Spider and Ace seem to have gone into a snickering contest, but I am not hanging around for more of this and make my way over to my trailer, muttering about insufferable alpha males along the way.

A couple of minutes after Brand, Ace, and Spider empty the truck's bed, they take off, and that leaves Shades and his team continuing here. I make myself comfortable back in the trailer with Coal and grab my laptop to work on the menus I want to put into place when I open.

I send a text to Spider asking for the contact information for his artist friend as I want to discuss the work, I could pass her way if she is interested.

I have nearly finished the menus when my cell starts ringing. I grab it without looking and am surprised when Stephen Woolcombe speaks, "Hi Pip, just thought I'd give you a ring and see how it's all going?"

"Oh hello, Mr. Woolcombe, everything is good, moving along nicely actually." as I am responding, my mind is racing, thinking what the hell is he ringing me for, I have only spoken to him a couple of times after my parents died.

"Good, good, it is nice to know all is going well. Have you thought about my offer to buy your shares?" he says, trying to be cool, I'm sure!

"No, I have not. My parents' Will was quite specific that they wanted me to keep my shares, and with my lawyer's advice, I'm going to do that, Mr. Woolcombe. I appreciate you are offering, but the answer is no, I'm not selling." I respond pretty coolly, thinking pushy fucker.

The line is silent for a few moments, and he then snaps, "You will sell to me, I want you out of the business, and I want you out quickly."

"I'm telling you, Mr. Woolcombe, I will not be selling my share in the company, and I'll make sure that my lawyer knows that too. I have made a new will myself, and my shares will not be going to you either." and I cut the call and sit staring at my cell.

I lied. I have not made a new will, but I will be doing that in the next couple of days as I have this uneasy feeling that something terrible is going to happen and going to be happening soon.

Opening the note app on my cell, I sit for a while jotting down ideas for my will, where some of my money could go, who I leave the company to, and Coal, my eyes tingle with the thought of not being here for him, I struggle to not cry at the thought.

Thinking about my few cross words with Brand, I have to smile at Spider and Ace's reaction. Maybe an alpha male is not used to someone saying no, well too bad as this woman knows how to say that.

CHAPTER 6

****BRAND****

Calling all Officers to Church has to be the way forward. Something's not right with Bruce Tailor, and we need to find out what that is before he creates a real problem for Pip or the club.

I check my watch to see another thirty minutes before our meeting starts. I lean on the bar and indicate to Dagger, our longest-standing prospect, to give me a beer. I glance around and see that a few of the brothers are in the clubhouse at the moment. A couple of the club bunnies that live in are hanging out too.

Ink wanders over and parks himself on the seat next to me. "Anything to worry about, Pres?" he asks quietly while he scans the room.

"No idea yet, but be alert at the shop for now at least," I respond. I lean nearer and quietly say, "This is about Officer Tailor, keep your ears to the ground, yeah?" I trust Ink but cannot tell him much as it's an Officer's meeting in Church, but I want him more alert.

"Will do, Pres." he grabs a drink and wanders off to watch the game with some of the old boys who occupy the far corner of the clubhouse. They are all harmless these days but can still pull a gun if needed.

Keely, one of the club bunnies, wanders over. "You okay, Pres, need anything?" as she runs a finger down my forearm and gives me that hopeful look.

Keely is about 5' 8" in height, long brown hair and a pair of fake tits that could poke your eye out if you were not careful, she has her sights set on grabbing an old man, but I am sure none of the men are going to go down that road. Nobody wants an old lady everyone in the club has had.

"Na, get to someone who wants a turn, I got shit to do." and with that, I wander off to Church to be ready for the meeting. I have a natural beauty in my mind of late.

As I'm waiting for everyone to turn up, my mind wanders to how quickly Officer Tailor moved back to his vehicle and drove off that first time he made contact with Pip. Something was a bit odd about that because we shouldn't have scared him away, but for some reason, us turning up didn't play into his plan.

Torch wanders in and plants in his seat, followed by Trigger, who sits next to me in the VP's seat. Patch, Tyre, Eagle, and Dollar come in all together and close the door behind them. Today's Church will be the seven of us.

The table has our club logo carved into it, done by my grandfather when the club was started. On this side sits Trigger, my VP, Eagle Club Secretary, and Dollar Club Treasurer. Everyone else sits in the same seats each time on the opposite side of the table.

"Meeting to order, and the only thing I wanna talk about is Officer Tailor and this problem with Pip," I state. "Does anyone have any idea as to why he is dogging Pip? Also, any clue as to who has been on her property?" Looking from one to another as I finish speaking.

Patch taps on the table with his knuckles. "I spoke to Ace about what he thought, and he's goin' to make sure the cameras are up in the next 48hrs. He told me there was no real evidence as to who had been on Pip's property as two cigarette butts were nothing to go on."

"Yeah, I spoke to Spider, and he wants the fencing up as soon as possible. He is going to put Whisky and Ice on extra hours if needed to get it done." Trigger says.

"Shoes is going to be doing some night duty to watch over the site and Pip, of course," I state. "But there's something not right because why did Tailor just buzz off when we turned up? That is not his norm. Something feels off," I look at everyone with an eyebrow raised wanting to know if anyone else thinks it is off. "Also, pulling her up twice, once for speeding and then the trumped-up drug charge. That had no way of sticking as the lawyer squashed him fast on that one."

"I agree with Pres, it was odd, and I'm going to talk to Spider about digging into Pip's background, see if anything stands out," Torch responds. "I also don't think she should be anywhere on her own for now, not until we know more, at least. Pip has to go to the warehouse to see about appliances next week, and that's an hour's drive. I don't think she should do that alone." Torch is our enforcer as he easily can put a beat down on anyone. He is 6' 5" and has a solid wall of muscle. He has this need to protect who he cares about and particularly innocent women and children.

"Okay, so we make sure Pip is not on her own for the time being. We dig into her background and see if, for any reason, she is being targeted by a cop. We also get the security in place as fast as we can. Is everyone agreed?" I state as I start to stand. I look around, and everyone nods.

Back in the commons, I head over to the bar and see Molly filling shelves and taking inventory. Molly is Trigger's old lady. She's a pleasant woman, chats to everyone, but I know she hates the bunnies in the club. I suppose most old ladies wouldn't want that type of woman around their man as we would not be happy if it were the other way around if we were honest.

"How are you doing, Molly? Everything good here with the bar?"

"No problems here, Pres. It's getting a bit difficult to man the bar as long as we need to. Trigger wants me to cut my hours back, but I don't think that's an option at the moment."

"Hmm, he hasn't mentioned it to me. Remind him to speak to me about it. We can maybe do something to lessen your hour's babe."

Before we can continue, Keely comes walking over again. I feel myself starting to getting pissed with her continuous attention. I also note Molly is getting tenser.

Once she reaches us, she runs her hands down my thighs, but I grab her wrists and move her away.

"I told you already I'm busy. Not interested, go service someone else or find a clubhouse chore to go do." I snap. She is far too persistent for my liking.

Sandy, another bunny, walks to the bar, gives me a small smile, and asks Molly if she needs any help as she has done all her chores and has time now before she has to go into the kitchen.

"You can help me wash that shelf of glassware Sandy, they have not been done for a couple of weeks," Molly responds pleasantly.

Keely is still hanging around, listening to anything said I notice.

"If you have nothing to do, Keely, I will find you a chore," I state waspishly. "We don't need you standing around here."

She huffs and stomps off, but I keep my eye on her for a minute or two. Taking herself off to the old boy's corner is not finding a chore to do. I need to speak to some of the brothers and see how lazy this little bitch has become.

"You alright Sandy?" I ask as she seems nervous today.

"Yeah, thanks, Pres. Just tired actually, seems to be a lot to do around here these days."

I note she is looking at Keely as she says this. Yes, I need to check out what she is doing or not doing, as, from this conversation, it appears that the other bunnies are picking up her workload.

With this fresh in my mind, I walk down to the security office and see Ace is working on something or another.

"Ace, do you still have cameras in the clubhouse?"

"Hi, Pres. Yes, we do, but we don't have them online unless something is amiss. Don't think we used them since we had that snitch four years back," he responds, turning in his chair to look at me questioningly.

"I need you to speak to Spider and between you two, work out what you need to do, but I want information on what Keely is doing around here. My gut tells me the others are doing her work, and all she is doing is walking around trying to look busy. Sandy looks haggard, and I know she works hard anyway, she doesn't service the brothers very much, but she earns her keep." I sit and lean my elbows on my knees. "If you can look into it fairly soon, I would 'preciate it."

Making my way to my room, I note Keely is still sitting and talking, doing nothing she should be, that is for sure. This is pissing me off, Sandy is still helping Molly, and I can see Pink is washing tables down in the dining area. I veer toward the kitchen instead of upstairs and look at the mess in the kitchen that still needs sorting. My jaw must tick as I'm not happy at all at this moment in time.

"Pink? Who's on kitchen duty?"

She walks over and tells me the morning duty was her and Keely. Cathy is upstairs doing bathrooms, and Sandy is afternoon/evening kitchen.

"So, if Keely is on kitchen duty, why is she sitting and talking?"

Pink blinks blushes, and turns away. This is precisely what I was worried about.

"KEELY, GET YOUR ASS OVER HERE," I bellow.

She saunters over, trying to look sexy, I think, but looks just what she is a nasty piece of work.

"What can I do for you, Pres?" she purrs.

"You can get your fuckin' ass in that kitchen and do your job," I snarl at her.

"Kitchen?"

Oh, she is going to play miss innocent. I don't damn think so.

"Yeah, the kitchen. You're in the kitchen this morning. The place is a bloody mess. Pink is working on her own here instead of with you, with who she's partnered. Get your lazy ass in there and get it done, alone. Pink has done more than her share."

"No, no Pres, I need her help in there," she whines.

"Well, she needed your help out here, but where were you? Chatting, fuckin' around, and not doing what you're supposed to be doing. Now get on or get out and I mean out the front door and not come back."

"You don't mean that?" she gasps

"Oh, for sure I do," and I turn to look around the room, see who is available. "Patch, you got a bit of time?" I shout to him

"Sure, Pres, I just finished what I had going on, so I have a couple of hours."

"Watch and make sure Keely does her jobs in the kitchen. If not, she's out," and I stomp off up to my room.

Once in my room, I grab a quick shower, get redressed, and sit at my desk looking at some figures Eagle gave me for the Fit & Fix business. We'll need to have some brothers to take over that place. I wouldn't say I like having outsiders running something in the club's name.

Tapping on the door, then Ace asking if I'm in and have a minute. "Come in, Ace."

"Sorry to disturb you, Pres, but I have asked around a little, and it seems you were right. No one has seen Keely doing any form of work. They have only seen her sitting talking, not even servicing anyone that they know of", he scrunches his nose up, which makes me grin.

"You not liking the idea of being serviced?"

"Not by her, I don't, she's dirty man, real dirty, she's had that many men on her no one will want her." he looks like he could shudder.

"Maybe time for her to move on. We need to bring it up in Church." I reply.

"Agree with ya, Pres, it's past time. She's not even like Sandy, who's putting in more than her share to earn her keep."

"Ok, tell everyone to keep an eye on her, make sure she does her share on the roster."

I tidy up my desk and head back down for a beer and maybe a game on the TV.

CHAPTER 7

####*PIP****

Thursday morning, the cameras are all up and working, thankfully. The fencing is one-third completed, which is excellent as it's a vast area. It covers the whole perimeter of the parking lot. The property plans show enough for eighty vehicles, not counting the bays at the back of the building for deliveries.

Patch, I find, a bit hard going as he never smiles. I have tried to get him to crack one, but as yet, not happening, but I'm not giving up. Nash, on the other hand, is fabulous. I can hear him singing nearly all day long, he ranges from country to rock, and he can sing. When he least expects it, I join in if I know the words.

Shoes and I get along well. He is sweet, somewhat shy, but intelligent. Yesterday I caught him on his cell looking at Forbes, and he's playing with the market but only with a few dollars. I suppose on a prospect's pay he doesn't have much to play with, but I'm going to get together a proposition and speak to him when it's just the two of us around. I don't want to make him feel embarrassed by risking any of the others overhearing.

I check my messages on my cell and see Spider has sent me the contact details for his friend Jenna, no time like the present.

Four rings, and it is answered. Before she can say anything, I jump in. "Hello, Jenna? This is Pip. Spider has given me your number. I wanted to talk to you about you doing some work for me if you'd be interested?" I blurt it out as quickly as possible because Spider told me she is a bit nervous about new people.

"Oh, hello Pip, Spider mentioned you might ring," she responds and sounds okay about me contacting her thankfully.

"If you could come out to see me, I could discuss all I need doing, and you can give me any ideas, but basically, I need a logo, business stationery, flyers, etc." I throw it out there so she has an idea of what is needed and if she will be interested.

"Yes, I'll come out next week if that's alright. I have your number now, so I'll send you a text of when and the time. Will that be alright with you?"

"Perfect, Jenna." and we close the call for now.

Looking at the time, I best grab something to eat and a quick drink. I'm going to the warehouse with Shades to select all the items we'll need for the building. I am excited, I have to admit, stoves, hot plates, food mixers, the list goes on, and I can see them all in my mind's eye how they will look fitted in the kitchen.

An hour later, I am eager to go. I lock up Coal, he'll be safe while I'm gone, and then I stroll out to see if Shades is ready to roll. Before I can get to the front of the building, he comes strolling around. He is a handsome man. 6' 4", black hair in a low pony, all muscle, stunning.

"Oh, I'm ready, can't wait. Do you want to go in my SUV Shades? You can drive!" I give him a grin as I know he has been ogling my beast, and as his SUV looks like it's ready for the scrapyard, I'm sure he will enjoy himself being in charge of mine.

"Fuck, yeah, Pip, I'll drive," he states as he's taking his kutte off and then drops it on the back seat.

"Why are you removing your kutte?"

"We never wear our kutte in a cage Pip, you'll see all the brothers remove them, and if not, they need a talking to." he doesn't explain any further.

The warehouse is an hour away, and I have to admit I enjoy the ride as not going anywhere and being under house arrest, as I call it, has left me a bit itchy to get out and about. The scenery is lovely. I enjoy being in the country and this small-town suits me well. I hope it's big enough to support the restaurant when it opens.

The warehouse is enormous, and it's a bit daunting when you see how much area we'll cover to get everything I need. I'm excited, and I don't know where to start. I grab my trusty notebook from my pocket and grin at Shades, who gives me a small smile and a nod.

Poor Shades is looking a bit sick four hours later when we finally have everything we need, double-checked, and then paid for. An excellent day as far as I see it, I'm not sure about how Shades feels, but he's been a good sport throughout this whole shopping experience. He never grumbled at all, although I could see he was getting frustrated at the time it was taking. Whenever I asked for his opinion on something, he quickly gave me an honest response which I appreciated.

We are about halfway home and chatting when Shades stops talking mid-sentence. I give him a curious look, but he is staring in the rearview. I twist around and see a black van coming up behind us fast.

Shades grabs his cell out of his pocket, hands it to me, and tells me to ring Brand and let him know we may need them to meet up with us on the road.

I find and hit the dial for Brand, and I hear him say, "You, Shades." and before I can say anything, the van hits us hard from behind, shunting us near the ditch.

I grip my seat and freeze as I don't know what to do as I don't want to distract Shades as he is fighting with the wheel to keep us on the road. I've dropped the cell and start to look to see if I can find it but daren't take my seatbelt off.

Shades shouts, "Hang on tight, Pip." and with that, I feel the hit from the van behind us, and we catapult down into the ditch, start to roll, and then all I know is blackness.

****SHADES****

"Pip, Pip, come on, wake up, you're gonna be okay," oh fuck, she has blood pouring from a nasty cut on the side of her head.

I have my seatbelt off, weapon out, and although we are upside down, I've lodged myself, so if anyone comes up to the driver window, I can shoot the fuckers.

I can hear nothing. It seems the bastards ran us off the road and then kept going. I maneuver myself to get a good look at Pip. She's still out. I want to get us out of here in case we have any leaks. We risk being blown up or burning alive.

Checking Pip as best as possible, I can't see how I will get her out through the driver's side and pull myself out.

Then thank God, she starts to stir. I stop her lifting her hand to her head. I don't want her touching the wound.

"Pip, you awake? Can you answer me?" I say this as I hold her head in one hand while I hang on with my other.

"Shades, are you okay?" Pip asks me, fucking hell, she is hurt and worried about if I am okay. This woman is such a good one, and if Brand doesn't pull his pants up, I will make my play.

"Yeah, I'm okay, babe. Can you climb out if I help you?" I'm still trying to keep my ears open in case the fuckers come back.

"Yes, I hurt, but if I can hold onto you, I can do it, Shades," she responds weakly.

After some effort, we make it out the window and up onto the side of the road. I sit Pip down and go back, grabbing everything that we need to save. Checking it out, the SUV stalling was a good thing as the engine cut off. It will have to be hauled out of the ditch as no way can it be driven out.

Sitting next to Pip on the side of the road, we hear bikes. Looking at each other, we know we have the club as backup now, thankfully.

Brand is off his bike and to us before we can stand up. Tyre, Torch, and Patch climb down to check out the SUV.

"What the fuck happened, Shades?" Brand shouts frantically.

"Black van rammed us a few times, and in the end, it pushed us into the ditch. As you can see, we rolled once," I respond. "Blacked out windows so I couldn't tell who it was or be able to identify anyone, but they had no plate, and that was what made me look twice when they came up behind me originally."

"Let me look at your head Pip, you're bleeding pretty hard." Brand asks. He gently lifts her hair and hisses at the nasty gash he finds.

A vehicle pulls up, and a middle-aged lady gets out. "Is everyone alright?" she shouts. "I'm a nurse if anyone needs attention!"

"Yes, we have a head wound here if you could look at it," I respond, much to Brands' disgust. He is giving me an evil glare. What the fuck.

I think Pip must have noticed as she has a little giggle, it's either that, or she's going into shock.

The lady cleans it up and puts steri strips on the gash, but she had to cut some of the hair around it, so that didn't please Pip or Brand in the slightest. At least it is cleaned and bandaged now.

Patch is on his cell and informs us he has a tow truck coming to pick up the SUV, and he's spoken to Cali to stay with Coal until Shoes turns up for his night shift.

Torch lets us know he has Spider bringing the club's SUV to pick us both up. No way am I riding bitch with one of them, I would never hear the last of it, and at 6' 4", I could hardly be inconspicuous about it either.

I note Brand is keeping his arm around Pip, not letting anyone get too close to her, fucker, I knew he was interested. Oh well, he is a good man and needs to get himself an old lady. I cannot wait to rip him one for being pussy whipped.

CHAPTER 8

****PIP****

Back at the trailer, Coal is excited I'm home, but he can sense something is amiss. He stays close to my side and on the alert.

My trailer seems pretty tiny with all the large bikers standing in it, and the looks they are giving me are making me feel nervous.

Brand sits opposite me and stares me straight in the eye.

"Pip, you've got to come and stay at the clubhouse for a few days till we can be sure you're safe. I know you don't want to, but it'll be the best way for us to watch over you. You can bring Coal. We can get your SUV insurance kicked in, too, get you set up again."

"No, not happening, nope, I want to stay here, I have Coal and Shoes is here patrolling at night, I have Shades, Cali, and the others in the team during the day too. I won't be run off my property, Brand." I stand and start to pace a little as I respond. I cannot go far as too many people in the trailer, although it is a large one.

"Pip, you need to do this for a few days. We can ask Shoes to move into your trailer while you're at the clubhouse, so the property has someone here 24/7, but you are at risk, darlin', and we don't want to see you get hurt more than you have been." Shades is trying to appeal.

"How long?" I ask, dammit, I don't like this, and I hate feeling I have been run off, but I am worried, and I was scared when that vehicle ran us off the road.

My cell starts ringing, and I grab it off the table where Torch dropped it when we came into the trailer. At a glance, I see it is Stephen Woolcombe again.

I click to accept the call.

"Hello, Mr. Woolcombe," but before I can say more, he jumps in nastily, saying, "Well, how are you, Pip? I hear you had a nasty accident! You up for selling yet?"

"No, I'm not, and I never will be selling to you, asshole," I shout and close off the call. He can kiss my ass. I will be contacting Larry later today for sure and putting a new will into place. I cannot delay it now.

When I look up, the trailer is full of the sight of angry bikers who heard every word and are no happier than I am.

"You will be coming to the clubhouse Pip, so get yourself a bag and get it done now. No way you're staying here until we work out what the hell is going on." Brand snaps.

From that point, everyone seemed to come alive, and I grabbed the basics of what I would need for myself for a few days and then the few bits for Coal. He knows by the aura that something is wrong. He is one step either behind me or beside me the whole time.

Once outside, I look around the property and see how much work everyone is achieving. I note a few extra workers building the fencing. Spider is pushing the security issue.

Torch wanders to me and puts his arm around my shoulders, pulling me into his side. He lowers his voice and says, "Come on, Pip, it'll be okay, we'll keep you safe, and anyone that tries anything I'll just beat the shit out of, how about that?" as Torch is 6' 5" and build like a brick, I have no doubt he could do that.

I couldn't help but look up at him and smile, "Yeah, Torch, that would be cool." I put my arms around his middle and hug him.

Then I hear it, a growl, I look down at Coal, but he is calmly looking around. I see Brand standing there giving Torch an angry look and goddammit growling at him. I glance back up at Torch as he steps away with his hands up at his sides, grins, and walks off. What the hell is going on!

Brand steps towards me, grabs my bag where I had put it on the ground and puts a hand on my elbow, and guides me to an SUV that the club uses. He stashes the bag, Coal and then myself into the vehicle and shouts a few orders to the men before we are on our way to the clubhouse.

The clubhouse is a short way toward town. It sits back from the road and has fencing and a large gate at the front. I see a prospect I don't know as we approach, but I recognize the prospect kutte he is wearing. He opens the gate, gives a chin lift to Brand, and a half-smile to myself.

Brand looks to me. "That's Dagger. He'll be patched in as a brother next month. He's been with us nearly a year. If no one is around and you need something, Dagger will do whatever he can and don't feel shy to ask."

I see a few bikes lined up in front of the building. It's a big place, looks like a warehouse from the outside, has been cleaned up, and has a large club logo on the wall above the main entrance stating 'Satan's Guardians MC.'

By now, I'm feeling a little sick as I'm hungry and need a drink, the knock on the head has caused a headache, and it is starting to rage. I can feel myself swaying, and as Brand helps me out of the SUV, I hold onto the side of the vehicle.

"You okay, Pip?" Brand asks as he gives me a good look over.

"I feel a bit dizzy, and my head is throbbing. I think I need a drink and something to eat since I have had nothing since first thing this morning," I reply with a grim smile.

Brand opens the main door, and we enter a small hall. I note a camera above the door in front of us. Brand presses a buzzer on the side of the door, and it unlocks with a loud click. Pushing it open and entering, Brand holds a hand to the small of my back.

The place is massive. A bar runs the whole length of one side of the room. Tables and chairs are dotted around that area too. On the opposite wall is a huge wall-mounted TV and couches facing it, with some older brothers sitting there looking back at us. Just before those couches are two pool tables with large lamps above.

At the bar, a stick-thin young woman with pink hair is wiping down the area but having a good look at us, trying to fill her curiosity. Coal leans against my leg as he can feel I'm nervous, he is trying to give me comfort, and one of the reasons I love this dog so much is that he is totally in tune with my feelings.

A young woman with long brown hair and boobs that are so big they cannot possibly be real comes wandering over. By the look on her face, she is trying to be seductive, but it sure isn't working, in my opinion. As she reaches us, she plasters herself onto Brand and shoves me to the side. It makes me take a couple of wobbly steps as I was taken by surprise. Coal starts to growl and show his teeth at this skank, and if it were left to me, I would let him continue.

Brand pushes the skank off himself and snaps, "Did I say you could touch me bitch? Get gone and do what you do best. Get on your knees for one of the brothers."

Oh no, this is not good. I can feel my color draining away at this little incident. Coal leans on me and licks my hand. I'm sure he knows I'm going to start a panic attack any moment. I don't want to be here, less now than I did before I walked in.

"Come on, Pip, I'll show you to your room, and I need to have a chat with you." Brand states. He places his hand on my elbow and guides me forward.

We go up a flight of stairs and down a corridor where we pass a few rooms. At the end of this corridor is another flight of stairs, and we go up them too. We pass four rooms and stop at the next.

Brand opens the door and guides me inside. It has a nice queen size bed, dresser, desk, chair, and another door to the attached bathroom. I expected it to be dirty and dismal, but nothing could be further from the truth. The furniture looks relatively new, and the room radiates fresh and clean.

Brand drops my bag on the end of the bed and indicates he wants me to sit. I glance at Coal, who jumps on the bed, circles, and lays down. Oh well, he's not stressed, that is for sure. I sit on the end of the bed and wait for Brand to spit out whatever he has to say.

"Some of the women you see here are what we call club bunnies. They live in. They are here to service the men. They are here voluntarily, and they can leave whenever they want to. They are paid for cleaning and looking after the clubhouse, they cook meals, and they get to live here free," Brand says as a matter of fact. "There are two old ladies at this time, Molly, who is Triggers, she runs the clubhouse bar, Alice, who is Tyre's, she has her own hairdressing business in town. Alice is a bit of a gossip, so if you want a secret kept, don't talk to her, she is a great person and will make a great friend if you want her to. Molly is just Molly, she is always busy, but if you want help or a laugh, she will always find time for you."

"Okay, will I meet Alice and Molly?" I ask.

"Yes, they'll be around later this evening. They usually turn up for a meal with their men a few times a week and knowing you'll be here. I'm sure they'll come to welcome you." Brand responds, looking at me as though he wants to say more.

"Do you think I could have a nap as my head is hurting?" I ask as I stand and move to open the door, hoping Brand will leave.

"I'm going to send Doc up to check the gash on your head, the nurse did a good job, but I think it needs looking at to see if you need actual stitches," he comments as he steps nearer to me.

Brand lifts his hands to each side of my face, lowers his face to mine, and lightly presses his lips to mine. He steps back, gives me his half-grin where his dimple pops out and leaves the room.

I plop down on the bed and touch my lips with the tips of my fingers and cannot stop the small smile that curves on my lips.

Doc is lovely, an ex EMT who has a friendly bedside manner. He checks out the gash on my head, cleans it up, and puts new steri strips on. He tut's at the way the nurse had cut the hair around the gash but tells me she at least cut as little as she could get away with. He advises I take some acetaminophen which he gives me, and gets a bottle of water out of his med bag, to which I look at him surprised. He laughs and tells me he knew I would need one, so grabbed it out of the fridge before he came up.

I lay down next to Coal and snuggle into him as soon as Doc leaves, and within a few minutes, I am fast asleep. I miss the fact that

Brand, Shades, and Torch have all looked into my room while sleeping to check I was alright.

A knocking on the door wakes me, and I call out to come in. To my surprise, it's Spider who enters.

"Hi Pip, I just wanted to see if you're alright and it's time for you to eat something," he says.

"Give me a minute to freshen up, and I'll come down. I want to let Coal out, so will you be able to show me where I can let him do his business?" I ask.

"No problem, Pip, I'll wait just outside your door for you," he says as he leaves the room.

Standing outside with Spider watching Coal sniffing around, I take some deep breaths of fresh air. My mind is running over everything that has happened today.

"You okay, Pip?" Spider asks, giving me a concerned look.

"I think so, Spider. A lot's happened in such a short space of time. I need to speak to Larry to have my will updated, the insurance on my SUV needs sorting, and something is seriously wrong with Stephen Woolcombe. We now know he is sending people to run me off the road to scare me into selling to him. But why, what the hell is he hiding that he wants me gone from the business?" I state.

"At the moment, I don't know Pip, but Ace is on the case. He's digging into what's going on with your parent's business practice, see if anything shows up. He'll look into Woolcombe too, and he can dig up anything, so I'm sure we'll know something soon," Spider replies. "Come on, Pip, the meal will be out now, so let's go eat." and he calls Coal as we turn to go in.

Oh my God, is this actual food or what. I am not sure what the hell it is. It is brown and a bit on the slimy side. No way am I eating this crap.

As I glance up and peer through my eyelashes, I can see the amused looks I am getting as my face must have said it all. I have never been good at hiding my feelings. I am positive everyone knows how disgusted I am.

One thing is for sure it will be a long time to breakfast, and I hope it's cereal as it cannot be ruined.

Molly is great. I hit it off with her straight away. She is chatty with a genuine happy-go-lucky attitude. I like her instantly, and sure we will get on well given time. You can see Trigger loves her. It shines from him when he looks at her.

Alice, I'm a little more reserved with, she is okay, but I would not have chosen her for Tyre, to be truthful. She digs for information as we talk, and I don't like that at all. I know Brand said she was a gossip, but I didn't realize she would be downright nosy. I am sure we'll not be besties as I don't like thinking before I speak in case what I say is repeated.

I am sure I am putting some noses out of joint as I am getting dirty looks from three of the club bunnies. Who cares? They can kiss my ass, and of course, Coal will bite theirs if they try to do something to me.

Another one of them called Sandy was lovely. She welcomed me when I came into the dining area, asked if I needed a drink or anything, and give her a shout if I did. She stroked Coal, and he didn't mind at all, which took me back a little as he is usually standoffish with people touching him when he doesn't know them.

A couple of the older guys came over and grabbed me in a hug. They were funny too, falling over each other to make the best impression. Thunder, who looks grumpy, is full-on hilarious. He had my sides aching with his antics. All in all, meeting them was a nice ending to my day.

CHAPTER 9

####*PIP*****

Waking in a strange bed is never good for me. I roll over and grab my cell, I check the time and see it is 4:00 am, but I am feeling well-rested. I get a shower, dressed, and call Coal, who yawns loudly and jumps off the bed, a huge stretch, lazy dog, but he makes me smile.

Once I have let Coal out and have the coffee pot ready, I grab a cup and sip at it while checking out all the kitchen area. It's nice, restaurant-quality appliances, and a massive island right through the center of the room with cupboards along one side, stoves, rows of shelves with pans sitting on them, and a fridge and freezer on the other side. I love this kitchen. To top it off, there is a big serving hatch that you can open up straight to the dining area.

Well, I am a chef. Hey, what made anyone doubt that I would not get elbows deep in something. I check out the cupboards, and at the end of the room, I open the door to a massive pantry. Oh joy, I rub my hands together. I double-check the fridge and find everything I need.

Sometime later, I have serving plates laying on the center island on warming trays I had found. Cinnamon rolls, biscuits and gravy, eggs benedict, bacon, sausage, scrambled eggs, and pancakes all lined up. I hope I didn't overdo it.

The kitchen door opens, and Torch walks in, taking deep breaths as he aims for the counter. I have to smile as he starts to rub his stomach, and I can hear it growling from where I am standing.

"Oh my God, Pip, this smells amazing. Do you want me to help you take it to the serving hatch before the troops all storm in? By this time, I'm sure they'll be waking up with the delightful aroma winding its way through the building." He says all this with a smile on his face.

And this is where Brand finds us carrying all the food across. He stands, taking in the aroma, and then gives me his half-grin and walks over.

"You didn't have to do all this, Pip, but it's much appreciated. It smells pretty damn amazing." all said while he wraps me in a hug.

"I was awake and happy to do it, my way of thanking everyone for all the kindness they show me," I respond. "Okay, let's eat, that swill last night was just nasty, so I'm starving this morning."

One by one, men appear from nowhere, pile up plates and find themselves a seat. It's quiet as no one is chatting. All that can be heard is cutlery tapping. It seems everyone was ready for a good breakfast.

Cleaning up the kitchen, I rinse dishes and place them into the dishwasher. Sandy, one of the bunnies, is helping to pass me all that she brings through from the dining area. It has not gone unnoticed that the other bunnies are nowhere in sight for the cleanup.

We are talking about nothing much. She's not trying to push for any information, which I am grateful for. She chats about day-to-day things, asks me about Coal, and offers to take him out if I get busy doing anything. Coal seems to like her; hence, I don't see a problem with that as I know he wouldn't go with her if he didn't want to.

"Do you have any idea what the meal is tonight?" I ask Sandy hoping whoever cooked last night will not be doing it today.

"It's my turn tonight," Sandy responds. "I'm not sure what to do, to be honest. I like cooking, but for so many, it gets hard as I often get the quantity wrong, so we have too much or not enough" she smiles at that, and it lights up her face. "I think the men get frustrated that we aren't more domesticated, to be honest," giggling at her own comment.

"How many will be here for meals if all turn-up," I ask her while heading toward the freezer to see what I can find.

"About forty I think, it varies because Molly and Alice don't always come and Shades drags some of his construction crew in if they have had a hard day and others may be off somewhere on club business," Sandy replies with a sorry I am not much help look on her face.

"I'll cook tonight, Sandy, if you'll help?" I ask her, and at the same time digging the meat out of the freezer to start defrosting. "We'll do lasagna, garlic bread, and a side salad and finish off with a few desserts. What do you think of that?"

"Flipping heck Pip that will be great," she replies. "I always make sure we have a selection of things in the fridge and freezer just in case anyone wants to try and cook. I'm going to do some cleaning now and will catch up with you later." all said as she is bustling away.

I call Coal from where he has found a nice cool spot in the corner and take off for my room. I want to ring Larry, check out the insurance on the SUV, and catch one of the security team to see if they have found any information on Stephen Woolcombe.

Larry was worried about what I wanted to put in my will, but as I stated to him, it's mine, and I'll do as I want with it, and I will more than likely change it a few times in the next year. I'm leaving my business to Liza and my shares in my parents' business practice to the Satan's Guardians MC. I can't help it. I have this massive smirk on my face at the thought of Stephen having to give annual payments to the club, and the more I think about it, the funnier it feels. Any funds I have in my accounts are to be split between Liza and the club. I feel better now I have this all sorted, and Larry assures me he will have this in place by the end of closing today.

I give Larry a brief outline of what is happening with Stephen Woolcombe, and he tells me to stick where I am and stay safe. He will inform his FBI friend Bill Forest of the threat to me and see if he can push him to make this more of a priority. We agree to keep each other updated.

Insurance was no issue either, they are sending me a new SUV to replace mine, and I only had to pay out a small amount toward it.

As I go down to the common room, I bump into Crank, and I ask where I can find the security team if they are here or have an office somewhere else. He tells me to follow him and guides me down a corridor to a large room at the end, where I find one heck of a setup. Screens everywhere, clicking of keyboards, headsets on, gee, it's like something out of a movie in here.

Spider and Ace are busy but stop to update me on what they've found, and I had to grab a chair and sit. I stare at them both while trying to get my brain around what they are telling me.

"So, you are saying that Stephen Woolcombe has been skimming the business of millions over the last few years. Millions my parents worked hard to earn. Is that really what you're saying?" spoken in nearly a whisper as I am stunned.

Ace steps over to me, squats in front of me, and holds my hands. "Yes, that is exactly what we have found. He has skimmed eight million that we have found so far in the last ten years. We have triple-checked, but his personal bank financials and the business accounts show he has been transferring money intermittently to try and stay undetected," He is looking at me closely as though he is trying to read my thoughts. "With the fact that he is threatening you to get you out of the company, we have doubts that your parent's accident was an accident, Pip."

I jump up from my seat, knocking Ace onto his butt in the process.

"No, no, no, no, no," I keep saying like a mantra. If I say it enough, it won't be true. I turn and quickly walk out of the room and make my way outside, taking deep gulps of air while tears start to fall down my cheeks. Coal appears and stands in front of me and is on full alert. He won't let anyone get near to me, snapping and showing teeth if they try.

I cannot get enough air, my head is starting to spin, and I see spots appearing before my eyes. I can hear people saying my name and Coal snarling and then nothing, total blackness.

****BRAND****

I can hear my name being shouted, and it sounds urgent. I pick up my pace and head in the direction of the back entrance bumping into Spider.

"Brand, you have to hurry. Pip has fainted in the yard, and Coal won't let us get near her," he states, then spins and rushes off back the way he came.

I take off after him but cannot understand why Pip would have fainted. Did someone upset her, hurt her. I damn well want answers.

As I get into the yard, I see Pip on the ground and Coal standing over her, obviously on guard, and he won't let anyone near her. This is impossible. He needs to stand the hell down as we need to help her.

"Coal," I say sternly, "Come here, boy," to which he stops and looks at me but doesn't move. "Coal come here," I say again with a touch of a growl in my voice. He takes a couple of steps towards me, then stops. "Coal get here," I shout this time, and he slowly walks to me with his ears down. I grab his collar and then hand him over to Ace, who bends down and quietly talks to him, trying to soothe him.

I rush over to Pip and see she is starting to come around. I help her sit and ask her what happened.

She tells me she spoke to Larry, the insurance, and then went to find Spider and Ace and the news they gave her.

I turn and give Spider and Ace a dirty look to let them know I am not happy with them, then help Pip to stand and take her into the common area.

Coal comes walking in from the yard and plants himself next to Pip, and I praise him as he did what he should do and protected her but responded to my orders when I gave them firm enough.

"Pip, we need to keep you here safe while we find out exactly what is going on. Obviously, that bastard is embezzling from the company, and we have the proof of that, but we need to know if he had anything to do with the accident killing your parents, and if he did, then we'll bring him down one way or another." I say all this, sitting next to her with one arm around her shoulders.

"Okay, Brand, I will stay here safe for now, I agree we need to know if he ordered their deaths and who he has working for him to run us off the road, but I'll need to talk to all the club officers soon to let you know what my new will stipulates," Pip says this while taking comfort with me holding her.

"Let Ace take you upstairs and settle you in your room for an hour, have a nap since you were in the kitchen from God knows when this morning." I kiss her forehead and hand her gently over to Ace.

As soon as Pip is up the stairs, I shout for everyone to get to Church.

It doesn't take long for everyone to pour in, and I tell Spider to update us on what they found.

"We hacked into Woolcombe's bank account and the business account, and found all the evidence that he has been transferring money over the last ten years that we've seen so far. From his account, he transfers to six other accounts, one of those being offshore. We have printed off the proof, and we're still digging to see what else we can find. We're also looking to see if any payments could have been for a hit on the parents and lately Pip." Spider relates everything as calmly as he can, but you can see from the pulse in his forehead that he is not as calm as he is trying to show.

"I have Chip, who, although runs guard duty for us, has been training on the research side on his off days. He's looking at all the accounts of the business to see if anything suspicious has been going on with a client," Ace supplies. "As of yet nothing, but he's only a third of the way through the files on the business system."

Spider once again speaks up "We need to think about putting a block on the business accounts, or this bastard is going to drain the accounts and run," He rubs his hand over his neck, shakes his head, and continues, "We know it would bring more heat down on Pip, but if we can block him, then the nine million in the business account will stay untouched at least, and Pip is 50% owner of the business, so she has every right to put a hold on the bank account by saying she wants a full audit completed, it would give us time. We can even get this Bill Forest involved if necessary once we know exactly what is going on."

I ask if anyone else has anything to add.

Shades states, "The fencing will be finished tomorrow as extra workers were brought in from town and the cameras were up and working fully yesterday. So, all told, we are on time still to get the restaurant up and running by the deadline if nothing else happens."

"With all the risks involved, we think Pip should stay here for at least a week, and then we'll have a full rotation of security running perimeter at the restaurant from the time she goes back. She gets on well with Shoes, so it's good that he can keep the night shifts for the time being if he does four on and two off for now. We can have Mallet step up too with Chip helping in the security room," Ace states. "We think that covers security at this point."

"Anything else?" I ask. "Nope, okay then, we will adjourn for now, and everyone be alert, report anything that looks slightly out of place."

I go into the common room and look for Thunder. Seeing him watching some rubbish on the TV, I stroll over and sit facing him.

"Thunder, I want to ask you to do something for me. I was hoping you could keep an eye on Pip when she's out and around the clubhouse. The bunnies are bitching quite a bit, and we all know how territorial they can be. I don't want them upsetting Pip any more than she already is," Thunder nods and responds, he can do that. "If anything happens, give me a buzz, and I'll get back here as quickly as I can. Thanks, brother."

"No need to thank me, she's a good girl. She smiles and nods at everyone. Her breakfast was pretty damn good too. I'm hoping she'll do more cooking while she's here," Thunder says all this with a grin on his face, then continues, "We need more old ladies now. Y'all are getting older and need a woman to keep you in line, could do with more kids too, only Ty here keeping us all on our toes."

"Yeah, I can agree with you, Thunder, but finding good women is the problem. We have so many patch chaser's these days it's like wading through water finding the good ones." I respond, shaking my head at the thought of the skanks that tend to want a bit of a bad boy.

CHAPTER 10

****PIP****

After my nap, I freshened up, had a quick stroll around the yard with Coal then decided it was time to get the meal organized.

Going back through the common room, I see Thunder and Crank chatting in the corner. I go over and ask if they can keep their eye on Coal if I tell him to lay with them. They were more than happy to watch him, and before I get in the kitchen, I look back and see Coal laid out on the couch with Crank. That boy, he sure gets spoiled, it's a real squeeze on that couch with his damn size, but by the looks of it, Crank doesn't care.

Sandy is making a fresh pot of coffee in the kitchen, just what I need after that nap.

Between Sandy and me, we grab what we need and get busy preparing the trays of lasagna. We are making six which are hardly small, and the trays are deep. I hope I defrosted enough meat to go around them. We get it all layered and ready for the stove within 40 minutes, which is perfect, and we place them on the side with towels over for now.

Sandy had the prospect purchase a huge shopping list, one we had written together and we grinned when we saw his face and the groan when he knew how much lifting he was going to do when he brought it back.

Next, we grab all ingredients, and I direct Sandy as to what to do to help me, and we soon have apple pies, oreo cake, pecan pies, chocolate brownies, and red velvet cake in or out the stoves. I am pleased that this kitchen has two restaurant-sized stoves as it has made it so much easier to get everything done.

"Okay, Sandy, let's have a cold one," I say, and we grab some fresh orange juice out the fridge. We are sipping our drink and washing up the old-fashioned way, yes, in the sink and not in the dishwasher, as I want the kitchen all clean and clear as fast as possible.

"Can I ask you, Sandy, without causing any hurt feelings, why you are doing what you do?" I honestly am interested, and if you don't ask, you never know the answer.

"Well, I was in foster care since I was 7. I was moved from one to another until I nearly reached 16, and I just decided enough when they wanted to move me again". Sandy looks sad, telling me her story.

Taking a deep breath, Sandy continues, "I ended up on the street as I had no money to pay for a place. I got hooked up with a young man who was also on the street, we became good friends, and we looked out for each other. We shared the food we had and any clothes we found worth having. I looked to him as a brother, but nothing was further from the truth in the end. As soon as I hit 17, he sold me to a dealer who dragged me to a room and locked me to the wall with a chain. Yes, I ended up a whore, not my doing, but a whore nonetheless" I see she has tears starting to fall, I grab her hand. "I escaped eventually, took me a year, mind you, and left that place behind as fast as I could. I walked for miles until I was exhausted. I was sitting on the side of the road when this biker pulled up. It was Whisky. He was kind, asked my story, and persuaded me to come here. To be a club bunny was my choice as I wanted to be able to contribute, and it was the only way I knew at the time." I squeeze her hand and then put my arm around her, showing her, I have empathy.

"Do you want to do this for the foreseeable future, Sandy? Or do you want to do something else?" I ask her as I have this idea forming in my mind.

"I would like to do something that is anything above a whore, to be honest. I had thought of going back to school, but I don't think I would enjoy that. My savings are growing very, very slowly, but once I get enough, I'm hoping to get my own place and a proper job of some kind. I always wanted to be an accountant as I am good with figures." she gives me a small smile while she's filling me in.

"Well, I have an idea. You tell me if you would be interested?" I state. "Once the restaurant is up and running, I will need staff, kitchen help, waitresses, and an assistant to help in the office. I would be happy to give you that opportunity, Sandy, and once my house is built, you could rent the trailer to live in. It's new, and it's large, it consists of a kitchen, dining room, lounge, bathroom, cloak, utility, two bedrooms, extra wide too." I am getting excited myself talking about this and start with a huge smile.

"Oh my god, yes, I would love to do that, Pip." and Sandy burst into tears.

"Oh, don't cry, this will be great, I know it won't happen tomorrow, but as soon as it can happen, it will," I try and calm her with my tone. "You would be a friend too, not just a worker, I only have one friend, and I would be thrilled to call you my friend too." and that is the god honest truth, I have never had friends as I was always too busy at college and that is where I met Liza.

"Oh, look here, we have happy hour going on. Don't tell me you're going to be a bunny too. I don't think that stick up your ass would help your case," all said with a nasty sneer by, of course, bitch of the week Keely and her sidekick, Cathy, who is standing there grinning too.

"All that said by the whore of the year. All you're good for is getting on your knees or your back. You sure have no brain. What are you going to do when the guys get fed up with your loose vajayjay, hmmm?" I spit out, I should have kept quiet, but I cannot stand this bitch. She is a real piece of work and why any of the bikers would want to dip into it is beyond me.

"You fucking bitch." she screeches as she rushes towards me, but before she gets to me, a voice spits out.

"Stop now, or you can get out and never come back. Pip is so much better than you and always will be. Maybe you could learn something about being a good woman if you took some notes!" Thunder furiously says. "Now get out of here before I kick your ass. I don't care if you're a woman or not."

"Thanks, Thunder, I appreciate you coming in and having my back," I state this as I am walking to him and wrap my arms around him for a hug. He pats me on the back and tells me any time, and he's happy to do it.

"What the hell are you cooking? It smells divine," Thunder says while taking a look at the counter and stoves.

"Oh, we have desserts baking, some out already, but don't touch," says I as I'm laughing at him. He looks like a little boy, his Ma scolded.

"I'll go sit back with Crank and wait patiently for mealtime then," he mumbles as he totters out the kitchen.

We get the last cakes out and cooling, and the lasagna is cooking. Next, we sort the frosting and cut up the breadsticks, and mix the garlic butter. All on time, although we had that small problem with Keely.

The kitchen smells fantastic though I say it myself. The desserts look fabulous, and Sandy did a great job as a helper too. She can follow instructions, and that will help her learn fast once the restaurant is open. All in all, this has been a good afternoon and just what my shattered nerves needed.

Brand comes striding into the kitchen, looking damn yummy. The last thing I need at the moment is a man. I have had one relationship, and it was hindered by him being all important and me having to rush around after him. Not again, not at this time either. I've enough on my plate.

"You made this kitchen smell like heaven again, Pip," he states as he goes to dab his finger into the frosting on the red velvet cake.

"Ah, ah, you do that, and you won't get a slice later," I say with my hands on my hips.

Brand laughs and asks if we're ready for the meal to be ushered to the hatch.

"All ready, we can get it moved over, and then everyone can help themselves," I state as I'm moving the first hot tray of lasagna over.

Well, I'm more than happy to say the lasagna, garlic bread, and the salad all was a huge success, everyone cleaned up their plates, and some of the men went back for seconds.

But I had to smirk when we brought out the desserts, pre-cut so everyone could get a serving. Thunder takes two pieces of Oreo cake and a slice of apple pie, giving me a huge smile and a wink when he did it.

"What is that about?" Brand asks me as he saw Thunder smiling at me.

"Well, he came into the kitchen and saved me from a problem with Keely this afternoon. I thought we were going to come to blows. She's a real mean one," I say this with no intention of causing trouble and realize that I dropped her in it. "It was okay though it was sorted, and I'm sure she will leave me alone from now on," I say this to try and defuse the situation, but I notice Brand is frowning and looking at Keely, who is sitting at the other end of the table.

"Who helped you do all this, Pip?" Brand asks.

"Sandy helped me, and I'm afraid I'm going to cost you her service when I open the restaurant up as I persuaded her to come work for me. She likes cooking, but she's good with figures and would have liked to do accounting, so we'll see," I say this timidly as I'm not sure what reaction I am going to get.

Brand grins at this and leans in to whisper in my ear, "Good for you Pip, Sandy is a nice person, and she deserves better than she has."

"Keely, you're on kitchen duty, and Cathy can help you do it. I want it spotless, and if I hear one word of complaint, you can find somewhere else to live and eat starting tomorrow." Brand states with what looks like a damn twinkle in his eye.

After we finish eating, I feed Coal and go out in the yard to let him have a run-around. I feel someone coming up behind me and turn to see who it is. Brand is walking up with a glass in each hand.

"Here you go, Pip, a cold beer to hit that spot," he states.

"Do you fancy a little walk up the yard so Coal can stretch his legs?" I ask Brand as I am a bit nervous at getting too far away from the clubhouse though it is fenced.

"Yeah," he replies and puts an arm around my shoulders.

We have a lovely walk up the yard, let Coal have a good run around, and then walk back down again. It was nice to pass an hour like that. We didn't talk much. I think we were both trying to stay off the topic of what my life has become.

As we get back to the clubhouse and before I can go in, Brand grabs my hand to stop me from walking.

"Pip, I like you, girl, I like how you are, how you portray yourself, and how you treat everyone. I want to get to know you and hope one day you'll be my woman," Brand says with all sincerity. I can hear it in his voice.

"I'm not sure it's the right time for me to think of a relationship with anyone Brand. But I do like you too, don't even think that I wouldn't jump at the chance if it weren't for all the shit that is happening to me right now," I respond. "Can we be friends for now? I would enjoy spending time with you, getting to know you, if that would be okay for now." I say this nervously as I'm sure he's not used to a woman holding him off, but I cannot get serious at this moment in time.

"Yeah, I'm happy to get to know you too, Pip. Many friendships turn into more." and he leans down and kisses my forehead. It is such an endearing thing that he does. It makes me like him more and more.

"Coal, come on, let's go," I shout, and as he trots to me, I turn again to Brand. "Night Brand, I'll see you tomorrow." and give him a small smile before turning and going indoors.

****BRAND****

I watch Pip walk in and feel relieved that at least I'll get a chance to know her and make her mine, but she has no idea she's mine already in my mind. Whether she likes it or not, I have this massive need to protect her. I knew as soon as I first saw her, she was going to be mine. I cannot explain it. It just is.

As I enter the common room, I look around to see who is still sitting about and see Glide, one of the old boys still watching TV. He's a grumpy old bastard, but he loves the club. We celebrated his sixty-eighth birthday not long back, but he looks more like he is in his early fifties. How he has managed that with the hard life he has lived is anyone's guess.

"Glide, you got a minute?" I ask as I walk over and take a seat next to him.

"Yeah, what's up, Pres?" Glide replies and turns the TV down slightly, keeping it just loud enough that our conversation is not overheard.

"Thunder is keeping his eye on Pip and the bunnies for me as I don't trust Keely and Cathy. Can you do me some checking with your mate in town and see if he has heard any rumors at all about Pip and the restaurant being built?" I also keep my voice down so it doesn't travel as I can see out the corner of my eye that Keely is still around and watching our corner of the room.

"I can do that, Pres. He turns in early these days, so I'll give him a call in the morning." He answers, and at the same time, his eyes are scanning the room, pausing on Keely as he passes. "Pres, I also think it's about time we got rid of the bunnies and just get paid help to do the cleaning. They are becoming more trouble than they are worth. Molly does great with the bar with Pink's help, and nobody taps Pink anymore. She's just not worth the hassle, she's a total airhead, but I know she would have nowhere else to go if we pushed her out. Keely and Cathy are just spiteful bitches who will eventually cause your woman more trouble." he holds his hand up to stop me speaking, "I know you well enough to know you got her under your skin already, Pres, but she would be good for you and the club, I would vote her as your Old Lady without hesitation."

I look at him a bit shocked, as I have never heard him say so much at one time. "Thanks, Glide, appreciate it. I'll bring up the bunnies in Church for a vote as soon as things settle down. We have so much going on with the construction, security for Pip, and the case we're building against this prick of a Lawyer that adding bunnies in the mix wouldn't be worth the time or bother."

I slap my hand on his shoulder and stand up, making sure I survey the room with my eyes as I do, and sure enough, Keely is still watching but trying to look as if she's busy chatting to Cathy. Yep, I am going to have to watch this pair.

I decide to wander down to the security office to see who is still working, if anyone. Chip is busy, has his headset on, so I tap him on his shoulder, making him nearly shoot out of his seat.

"Shit Pres you scared the crap outta me," he says but grins while saying it.

"How you doing Chip, find anything new?" I ask.

"Yep, found four of the accounts that Woolcombe has set up, so we can go in at any time now and remove his dollars," he says this with a damn grin on his face, and I'm sure he would be rubbing his hands if I wasn't standing here with him.

"I'm hoping to have the fifth and the offshore information by morning, so Ace can do a final tally of how much this thieving bastard has taken and for how long," he replies.

He's obviously enjoying his job from the laughter on his face.

"What about paying someone to do the hit? Any idea on that yet?" I ask, as this, I think, is how we will stop at least one of the threats.

"Yeah, I have an account number that $50,000 was paid into three weeks ago, but the money was cashed out, and the account closed within 24hrs. The ID on the account is false, so as yet no further information on finding who this is. Sorry Pres, I will keep digging." he replies.

"Okay, Chip, great job so far," I respond and give him a head nod as I leave.

Going back to the common room, I look around for Dollar but don't see him anywhere but don't see Sandy either, so he's probably gone off to his room to get him some. I must remember to catch him tomorrow and, with that, take myself off to bed.

CHAPTER 11

####*PIP****

For the last ten days, it has been a case of getting up, cook breakfast, potter around, afternoon cook meal, evening potter around. I've had enough. I want out of here. I want to see the restaurant which Shades informed me is nearly completed, and they have worked so hard to get it finished. The apartment hasn't been started as yet, but the main business had to take priority.

After breakfast is made, I get myself dressed warmer and grab my keys for my new SUV, which I have had no chance even to drive. I call Coal and make my way out the front.

"Whoa, Pip, where ya going?" Glide shouts, doing his best to catch up.

Awe shit, I just wanted to sneak out and be done with it. Surprise, surprise, no luck, it's like I'm under house arrest.

"Hi Glide, I'm going to the restaurant to see how it looks. I need to get the hell out of here for a while." but I keep walking to my vehicle as I shout back. I glance over my shoulder and see he's texting. Oh no, I know Brand or someone will be up my butt in a minute if I don't shift it. So, I do a mad spurt to my vehicle, call Coal to get in, slam the door behind him and quickly hop into the driver's seat.

I press the start button and put her in gear. I pull out the parking spot and head for the gate, thank God it's open, but I can see one of the prospects look down at his cell, oh no, not happening, and I put my foot down and get out that gate when I look through my rear view, I can see the prospect waving his arm and shouting to me. I don't care. I have a smile on my face, I am off, and no one is stopping me.

It's not far to the restaurant, so I make sure I watch for that damn cop and anything else that could be classed as suspicious. I know what I've done is wrong, but I can't stand being locked in the clubhouse anymore.

I pull into the parking area behind the restaurant, and oh, oh, I see Shades and Cali storming towards me.

As I get out of the SUV, I open the door for Coal to jump out, turn and shout, "I know, I know, but I couldn't stand it anymore. I'm not sorry; I just felt like I needed to escape and smell the fresh air. To come and see how everything is going."

Shades looks like he is going to blow a gasket, damn he is red in the face. Cali has his usual smile, and I think he is finding me being in trouble rather amusing.

"What the fuck were you thinking, Pip?" Shades, shouts at me. "You got a damn death wish or what!"

"Look, Shades, I am not a bloody prisoner. I needed out. I was dying of boredom," I said with my hands on my hips and, yes, getting an attitude. "You're not my father or my brother, or my damn jailer. If I want out, I am out, end of."

Oh boy, five bikes just tore into the parking lot, and I see Brand straddling his bike with a look of murder on his face. That is it. I am out of here.

I take off towards the trailer at one heck of a lick, Coal barking and chasing as he thinks it is a damn good game, and I can hear Brand shouting to stop, but no way am I stopping. I make it to the trailer, yank at the door, and shit, it's locked.

****BRAND****

Sitting with Ink at the tattoo shop, I'm having a peaceful morning when my cell dings twice. I take it out of my pocket, and I see two text messages have been sent. I read the messages, one from Glide and one from Billy 'The Kid', prospect on the clubhouse gate today.

I see red, jump out of my seat and take off for my bike. I place my helmet on, and while doing so, shout to Ink to get Patch, Trigger, Torch, and Tyre to the restaurant.

I take off down the road, and thankfully it's not too far as the shop is only on the edge of town. As I pass the clubhouse, four bikes are just leaving and tuck in behind me.

As I reach the restaurant, I go around back and start to park up, looking all the time to see if everything is okay, which it seems to be. I am still straddled on my bike, taking my helmet off when I see Pip. She takes one look at my angry face and runs for the trailer.

"What the fuck Pip!" I holler at her. "Come here and tell me what the fuck you were thinking?"

She reaches the trailer, but it's locked as Shoes will still be sleeping as he has been on duty for the last three nights. That gives me an angry smirk; I have to admit.

I start striding toward her, and she must be able to see how angry I am as she starts backing up and looking where she can run to or hide, which is nowhere.

"Okay, okay, Brand, I'm sorry, I was bored. I wanted to see how the work was coming along, you all have things to do all the time, and

I am stuck at the clubhouse." Pip's obviously trying to wriggle out of trouble.

Now I am only a couple of steps in front of her, and every step forward I take, she takes one back. Coal, for some reason, is dancing and prancing around, thinking this is a damn great game we're playing, but thank God he isn't trying to fucking bite my ass.

Just as I open my mouth to speak again, I hear a pinging noise. Pip screams and grabs her arm. Everyone jumps into action, guns out and aiming onto the back property. I grab Pip and rush her around the other side of the trailer out of the line of fire.

I know the guys will deal with the situation without me having to give orders. I take a minute to check out Pip, and she has a bullet graze over her right arm, not serious. Thank God, dammit, it's a good job she was still taking steps away from me, or she could have been killed.

"Pip, what the hell were you thinking?" I am trying to stay calm and get Pip to understand how serious this is. "This is exactly why you were supposed to stay at the clubhouse where we know you're safe. Until we get the evidence and catch whoever this is and get Woolcombe under arrest for putting a target on you, you have to stay where they can't get to you."

"I'm sorry, Brand, I was bored out my head. I like looking after everyone by doing the meals, but I just wanted to see how everything was going. Once I have meals done, I have nothing to do, and it drives me crazy as I am so used to being busy all the time." Pip responds she's is hurting and has tears running down her cheeks.

"Come here, Pip," I say and wrap my arms around her, giving her the comfort she needs at this minute in time. "It's a good job you're not my old lady yet, or you would be over my knee with a red ass," I tell her with, I must admit, a hint of fun in my voice.

Trigger comes around the corner of the trailer and asks if we are ok. I explain Pip has a graze where the bullet scraped her.

"He ran as soon as he took the shot, but I think I recognized him. I think it was Cole Barker," Trigger states. "I'm going to go into town and do some recon, see what I can find out about that little shit. I'll let Doc know you're on your way back." and with that, he takes off.

"Come on, Pip, let's get back to the clubhouse, get you safe and cleaned up" Brand takes my elbow and guides me toward my SUV. "Cali, will you get my bike back later? You can put it in the back of the trailer."

I place Pip and Coal in the SUV and then have a quick word with Shades to give Spider a call and see if we caught anything on the cameras. My priority now is to get Pip back and seen by Doc.

****PIP****

Back at the clubhouse, I am having my arm cleaned up and bandaged. Thankfully it is not a deep scrape, but it is giving me some pain.

"Pip, I can put cream on it and a clean bandage every morning if you come down here first thing." Doc is such a gentle person when he is in his Medic role.

"Okay, Doc, thank you," I ask him. "Can I have a couple of pain meds, and then I'll go have a rest for a while."

After taking the pain meds, I wander to my room. I thought Coal would be there, but he isn't, so I take myself off again to find him.

He isn't in the common room either. Panic starts to curl in my gut. Where the hell is he?

"Coal," I shout, carrying on walking through to the kitchen. No, he's not here either.

"Where's my dog? Where's Coal" I shout to anyone that is listening.

"Pip, calm down. He's out in the yard with Brand. He took him out before bringing him up to your room. No one would hurt him, babe." Crank advised. He knows how attached I am to him and that I don't like him away from me for too long.

Brand and Coal come into the common room, and Brand waves his hand, indicating to go back upstairs. As I go up the stairs, both of them are behind me. I can hear Coal puffing, so he has had a good run by the sounds of that.

When we enter my room, Coal jumps straight on the bed and throws himself down. Brand closes the door but stays standing there.

"Pip, you can't do this again; you have to realize how dangerous that was," he states.

"I know Brand, and I'm sorry, I just needed to get out of here for a while. I need my life to move on. I can't wait forever to get my life back." I reply, but I am upset, and I can feel my lip wobble as I try not to cry.

"I know, Pip, we're doing everything we can to get this figured out. We have a lot of information now and just need to get ends tied up, so we have that bastard Woolcombe in knots. Now we have to find this fucking shooter as that came way too close for comfort." Brand states as he comes to me and puts his arms around me for a hug that I have to admit I desperately need.

"Okay, Brand, I'll stay here for now and just hope we can get this wrapped up. But I do need to go to the restaurant as I need to know how close we are to being finished. I have to order all the pots, pans, cutlery, blah, blah, you understand? And then, of course, I'll have all the perishables to get before we open, so I need time to sort all that." I tell him, still feeling frustrated.

"Have a rest, Pip, and I'll fetch you at mealtime," Brand states.

"Oh, shit no, I am not eating that swill your bunnies cook, it is disgusting, who knows what they have done to it. I will have an hour and then come down. Can you ask Sandy if she will help me although it isn't her day, I don't think? I won't work with the bitch squad for sure." I tell him.

"Okay, will do, Pip," and he kisses my forehead and leaves.

*****

Time passes, and I wake up feeling somewhat refreshed. My arm aches a little but not bad, thanks to the pain meds Doc gave me to take. I clean up and get changed, and contact Jenna before checking out what can be done for mealtime.

Grabbing my cell phone, I find Jenna's number and give her a ring.

"Hello?"

"Hi Jenna, it's Pip. I'm sorry we didn't get together earlier. Things happened, and I couldn't make the arrangements with you. I still want you to do the work if you're interested, and I did a few doodles of my ideas for a logo for letterheads. Can I email them to you?" I quickly say to her, I don't want her to cut our call.

Jenna agrees we can do it that way, and when she has some ideas, she can email them back to me, and we can go from that point. So, we leave it at that for now, and I will look forward to seeing her ideas.

As I am heading for the kitchen, Sniper calls me over to the old boy's corner. I smile and wander over. He's sitting with Glide and playing cards, poker by the looks of it.

"You okay, Sniper?" I ask him while giving a warm smile to Glide.

"We're okay babe, how are you? Don't do that to us again, Pip, you frightened the shit outta us, and we're too old for that," he laughs while Glide is nodding agreement. Although, I can see the seriousness under his comment.

"I promise I won't." The last thing I want to do is worry them. "Let's just call it a moment of madness, and I learned my lesson," I respond as I want to put their minds to rest.

"Anything special I can make for you today?" I ask, and both of their faces light up at the question.

"Do you have any fruit in the kitchen, Pip? If you do something like blueberry muffins would be good or strawberry and vanilla cake." Glide quickly says while Sniper is nodding it's okay with him too.

"No problem, I will see what I can do," I answer with a huge smile. "Can you give Coal a run outside and keep him with you while I'm busy, please?" I ask, and Glide agrees and takes off with Coal beside him.

I see someone has been shopping as the fridge is full and has some joints that have not yet been placed in the freezer. So, I grab a large piece of ham, and beef and get them quickly in the stove. They are massive pieces of meat, so they need plenty of time to cook. Thankfully someone had at least put the stove on to warm up.

Sandy appears, and we both get busy preparing vegetables as I will roast them with mashed potatoes coated with butter and back in the stove to crisp up the top. Once this is all prepped and ready to cook a bit later, we get started on desserts.

Yes, I make blueberry muffins, strawberry and vanilla cake, peanut butter cookies, oreo cake as it went down so well last time, and to finish off, I did walnut and orange cake.

The good thing about cooking is the time passes quickly. Sandy and I chat about anything and everything and get to know each other. I am sure she will be a great friend and welcome addition to my staff when I get the restaurant open unless I can persuade her in time to do accounting.

"What the fuck are you doing? It's our turn to cook bitch," Slut of the year Keely shouts.

Oh, for god's sake, here we go again. This woman just does not know when to shut the fuck up and mind her own business.

"Well, you cook for yourself, that's okay, and we're cooking for everyone else," I state with a poker face I learned to do when at catering college.

"Keely, we are cooking. If you don't want to eat it, you don't have to. Brand told Pip she could cook whenever she likes, so if you have a problem, take it up with Brand," Sandy responds while having her hands on her hips and looking pissed, which I have never seen on her before.

"Get out of the kitchen," Keely shouts, "We'll finish this and take the credit for it," she says with a sneer.

"Hardly, how would anyone believe you cooked this when all your meals a pig won't eat," I state.

"You bitch" she says and runs at me, throwing a punch.

Well, I was ready. I have met idiots like this one before. I grab her wrist, twist it around, and swing her arm behind her back, at the same time grabbing her hair at the base of her neck. Hence, she cannot move now. It doesn't stop her mouth from moving, unfortunately, though.

Cathy, her buddy, takes offense at my restraining her and screams, charging at me, but Sandy steps in and slaps her hard, sending her flying across the kitchen. I see a lovely red handprint showing already.

The kitchen door flies open and Ace storms in. He takes in what is happening and lifts his eyebrow at me. "What the fuck is going on here, Pip?" Ace asks.

Sandy jumps in before I can speak.

"Bitch one," pointing at Keely "and bitch two," pointing at Cathy, "came in asking what we thought we were doing and when we said they didn't have to eat this and could make themselves something, bitch one said no, we could get out the kitchen, and they would take credit for our meal. When we told her to fuck off, she attacked Pip, when Pip restrained her, Cathy attacked, so I took her down," all said by Sandy in one breath, and now she's red in the face and glaring at the pair of bitches as she calls them.

I couldn't help it. I started to giggle. Keely began to struggle, so I hoisted her arm up even further, making her screech.

"Okay, Pip, you can let her go now," Ace states while taking hold of Cathy's arm and coming to take hold of Keely.

I only let her go because Ace was going to get hold of her, but before he could, she whirls around and punches me in the face. She catches me right under my eye across my cheekbone. Before I can retaliate, I see a flash of black, and Coal hits her in the chest, and down she goes. He has her pinned to the floor and ready to rip her head off. He's showing every tooth and all his gums as he's snarling that much.

The kitchen door flies open again, and pandemonium ensues. I call Coal off as I don't want anything to happen to him. I walk over and grab some ice, wrap it in a towel and walk out into the yard with Coal.

We wander over under one of the trees, and I sit on the bench while Coal lays next to my feet. I scratch behind his ears and tell him what a good boy he is.

Sandy strolls out the back door when she sees me, comes over, and sits down. She asks if I'm okay and tells me that the two bitches are in Church having their fates decided. She tells me Brand is furious, Ace is spitting fire and all four old boys want to shoot them. She says the last while giggling. I look at her, grin, and then can't help it, the visual I have of the old boys just does it, and I burst out laughing. That is how Brand and Ace find us, sitting on the bench laughing with tears running down our faces.

Brand informs us that Keely and Cathy were banned from the clubhouse and can't step into any of the club businesses. They cannot consort with any club member and will be run out of town if they do. If any club member or their old lady does not uphold this club decree, they will lose their patch or rights to attend the club.

After all this, we had a great meal, with everyone chatting and laughing. The atmosphere in the club seems to have lifted, which says a lot about how those two women were depressing everyone.

Pink was sitting at the table eating too. I wonder if she was having trouble with the other women? It seems strange that she was grabbing something to eat and disappearing before this.

All in all, I think the day ended well for everyone, and as I head off to bed, I notice members sitting watching TV and others playing pool. Great to see as everyone had been quite reserved before this.

CHAPTER 12

****BRAND****

The last week, thankfully, has been relatively uneventful, we've not found Cole Barker yet, but it has been confirmed by looking into his financials, Officer Bruce Tailor paid him. We know he paid $20,000 for Barker to take out Pip. Thank God he is a lousy shot.

When I think of how Pip has been cooking up a storm this last week to stay busy, it makes me smile. Fantastic meals and desserts have been laid out daily. The old boys now have Pip as their favorite person and have taken to putting requests in for desserts their Momma's used to make. Pip takes it all in her stride and is spoiling them rotten. It makes me smile, I'm glad she fits in so well.

She is unbeknownst to herself becoming the President's old lady and doing a fine job of it too. When I get to the point where I can claim her, I have no doubt the club will vote for her position as an old lady and protect her without a second's hesitation.

Grabbing my cell, I send a group text to call Church in 90 minutes. It's time we looked at all the evidence and make a timeline if we can of what has and is happening. Also, we need to get the vote for Dagger to get his full kutte and membership of the club.

I see Odds entering the common room, so give him a shout to come over to where I am sitting near the bar.

"Can I have a few minutes, Odds, or are you busy?" I ask.

"No, I got a minute for you Pres, what can I do for you?" he replies as he grabs himself a seat.

"How is the Gym shaping up? I know it's early days as you've only been open about nine months, but it seems all three of you are keeping busy, which is a great sign," I ask while indicating to Molly, who is cleaning behind the bar, that we could do with a drink, and pointing to the coffee pot.

"Gym is doing great actually," he responds, "We have classes running every day now for general fitness. Nights we see more serious types for MMA, Krav Maga, Jujitsu, we are also getting some inquiries about Boxing."

"Yeah, that's pretty damn good for the time you've been open," I reply.

"We're a bit stretched with just the three of us, but I don't want to get outside instructors. I'm looking at Billy 'The Kid' as he's doing some serious training a few times a week, I think I can mold him into what I want, but I need to bring it up in Church first." he says, looking to see if I will agree or not.

"I'd vote for that Odds, 'The Kid' is blending in well, he has been here about five months now, and he does as he's told, when he's told, I think he's going to be a good brother," I respond "We do however need to be on the lookout for new prospects as we'll be down to three once Dagger is voted in."

"I'll keep my ears and eyes open, Pres. We have some good lads coming in the gym now. Maybe I can pick us a couple up." he replies while getting up and walking off. "I'll be in Church Pres. I've just got to run an errand," Odds shouts.

****PIP****

Finishing up the kitchen clean-up from breakfast, I look over at

Sandy and ask if she can manage some cupcakes, muffins, and cookies for the meal tonight. Sorting that leaves me a bit of time as I need to talk to Larry about what happened and what he has to tell me from his contact Bill Forest of the FBI.

I make sure Coal is still with the old boys and indicate to them I am going upstairs. Glide gives me the thumbs up, so I jog up the stairs to my room.

Looking at my notepad, I make sure I have everything on hand that I need to tell Larry and ring his private number. I don't want to go through his office as I don't trust anyone at the moment.

"Hi Larry, it's Pip. If you have time, I want to update you on what is happening here," I say as soon as he picks up my call.

"Hello Pip, I was going to ring you later today as Bill is going to come down and see you. He's done a bit of digging and wants to put all the eggs in one basket, so he knows how to move forward," he says.

"Oh, okay, Larry, I'll wait and speak to him then. Is he coming to the clubhouse where I am staying now, or does he want to meet at the restaurant?" I inquire.

"I think it best he come to the clubhouse as it's not safe for you away from there at the moment," he responds. "Give me the address, and I'll pass that on and your cell number."

I give him the details and update him on what has happened with the shooter and him being paid by Officer Tailor.

I need to make a shopping list next and get one of the prospects to make a trip into town. All these mouths to feed goes through supplies fast.

I need to talk to Brand about more help to clean and cover the kitchen once I get the restaurant open. Because Sandy will be gone, which only leaves them Pink of the club bunnies, and I have to admit that makes me smile. We will need two or three cleaners as this place is massive and two for the kitchen, or we need to be looking at five that can cover wherever needed and not because of the size of their chests either.

Going down, I notice the place is empty, so I wander over to Molly, who looks like she is getting ready to leave.

"Hi Molly, you getting ready to go home?" I ask as I take a seat at the bar.

"Yeah, I am, all done here for now," she replies with a smile. "We're going to need help now you got shot of two and then Sandy will be going at some stage, which means three helpers gone," she says laughing, "I wish I had been here. I would have loved to see Keely get what was coming to her."

"I know, right. I didn't even try that hard either," to which we both burst out laughing.

"I have to talk to Brand about helpers Molly, so do you want me to add bar staff to my list?" I ask while opening my notepad again.

"Yeah, that will be good Pip, we need three really that rotate around bar times, but I think if we had new prospects, it could be added to their duties rather than women coming in again," she says, and I have to agree it would be a better solution.

"Okay, Molly, I'll do that and get back to you later or tomorrow when you're here, catch you later," I say as I am walking to the kitchen to check up on Sandy.

"You doing okay in here, Sandy?" I ask, checking out what she has managed to get finished.

"Yeah, Pip, I have nearly finished, cookies and muffins are cooling, and cupcakes are nearly ready to come out of the oven," she replies. "Anything else you want me to do?"

"Let's get those joints out to rest. They will cut better after standing a while," I respond while getting myself a cold drink.

Vegetables are ready to go in for roasting, but I do a large salad bowl to go on the side if anyone wants any. Some of them love salad which surprises me.

Sandy goes into the laundry room to finish up in there, and I take off to see if Brand has finished Church yet.

****BRAND****

Everyone is now in Church, and I make sure that Dagger is here too. He looks a bit confused as prospects are not usually allowed in Church.

"The first thing I want to cover in this meeting is Dagger," I make sure I pause, building up his worry a bit by giving him a look and raising my eyebrows. I know it's a dick move, but I cannot help myself. "I want to bring it to the table that Dagger has done his time, and I put forward he becomes a full brother. Who will second?" I ask while looking around.

"I'll second," Torch says, which is a high recommendation as he is our Enforcer, meaning he has checked out everything to do with Dagger and found nothing to cause the club any issues now or in the future, he also works close with Ace regarding prospect background checks.

"Okay, let's go round the table. It needs to be a unanimous vote," I say.

One after another, around the table, everyone votes for Dagger to be a fully patched member.

"Dagger welcome to the brotherhood," I say as I give him a hard smack on his back, making him take two staggering steps forward.

All the brothers do the same, welcome him, and give him the same smack on his back that I did. It's not ruined the grin on his face, although his back will be giving him hell.

"You book in with Ink to get your club tattoo as soon as possible, Dagger," I state. "Also, see Dollar about getting your prospect status updated to full kutte member. Now sit your ass down so we can get down to more business."

Over the next seventy minutes, we look at the connections we have found so far in Pip's case. We can see that Cole Barker was paid by Officer Bruce Tailor, and now Chip informs us that Officer Tailor is, in fact, cousin to, you guessed it, Stephen Woolcombe. *Kerching*, things are starting to come together.

We still haven't found Cole Barker. He seems to have disappeared off the face of the earth. Checking his financials, Ace sees the money has not been touched yet, which is strange as the word out there is that he has a massive gambling debt in need of immediate payment.

Spider has found one offshore account for Woolcombe and has managed to hack into it, so when we need to, we can empty that account.

Our primary concern now is Officer Bruce Tailor and getting him off Pip's back so she can get her restaurant up and running.

Ace speaks up, "We've found that Stephen Woolcombe started embezzling eleven years ago. His wife left him and then divorced him, which was ruled in her favor as she had evidence, he had a mistress. That was the start of his downfall financially as once the ex-wife cleaned him out. The mistress took the rest, even emptied his two properties with everything she could take in one day," He looks around at all of us. "He then took to gambling and smoking weed which has progressed to more substantial narcotics."

"So, he started taking the money to pay for his debts and drugs? Is that what you're telling us?" I ask.

"Exactly, Pres. From what we can see, it looks like Pip's parents found out and tried to help him, but instead of taking that help, he tried to make them look dirty and started planting lies about them," Ace continues. "I spoke to their secretary June, who is still working for Stephen Woolcombe, and she told me she is collecting evidence of what he's been doing. She has copies of bank statements and emails from him to Bruce Tailor. Bloody idiot's not taking any care at all to cover his ass."

He brings over a folder which he places in front of me. "This is what June has forwarded to me so far. We now have more proof we can give to the FBI Agent when he gets here to see Pip. It looks like Woolcombe is financing a drug house of all things and then selling to one of the cartels."

I run my hand over my head and down my face. This is just getting worse and worse, we don't want to go to war with a cartel, but we will, if we have to, to protect Pip.

"Any news on when Bill Forest of the FBI will be here?" Tyre asks sarcastically. He hates the FBI after having dealings with them in the past.

"Pip has not said anything as yet, but I'll ask her to set it up so we can move forward with this. In the meantime, we need eyes on Tailor and keep eyes on him. Any ideas on this because he knows all of us? We need someone outside the club if possible." I state.

"My brother Rip can do it," Dagger states. "He's working in town at the Gray Pony Bar, he hates the boss, and if we can give him the same wage, he can watch him without being seen. I've been speaking to him about prospecting, but he wanted to wait and see if I became a full brother first. Now I am. I can bet he will be all in."

"You all on board with that?" I ask.

Everyone gives me an "Aye," so I say, "Okay Dagger, get him over here as soon as possible, do it at night, make sure you're not followed or seen. Once we have him on board, we can get this ball rolling." Looking around, everyone is nodding in agreement. "Okay, let's call it done for now," I state.

Coming out of Church, I make my way out to my bike and take off for the restaurant as I want to see it now that it's finished. I also want to go up to the apartment and see if they've started ripping it apart. Construction is doing well, and I'm proud of all of them.

CHAPTER 13

****PIP****

Everyone is out of Church and gone off to do what they need to do. Darn it I missed Brand, so I'll have to wait until later to get his approval on finding help.

I make my way over to the old boys, plop myself down and ask if anyone fancies a walk up the yard. I see Coal is flat out once more. He is getting lazy with all this sleeping with these four.

"I'm up for a wander with ya, Pip," Thunder responds, getting to his feet and calling Coal off the couch.

Once in the yard, we take a nice steady walk up the perimeter fencing. We don't even talk, just enjoy each other's company.

Then I hear Thunder grunt. I look at him and see blood oozing through his jeans on his right thigh.

I grab his arm and pull him around a tree, and we both take what cover we can. I shout for Coal to come to me to get him out of the line of fire.

Thunder grabs his Springfield XD from under his kutte and tells me to stay down as he moves to engage the shooter. As soon as he clears the tree, I hear another grunt; he spins around, drops his weapon, and grabs his left arm.

"Thunder, get your ass back here," I shout to him.

Once he is next to me, I push him, leaning back on the tree. I see he has been shot a second time. He has beads of sweat on his forehead, so I know he is in a lot of pain. I grab his hand and squeeze it.

I carefully look around the tree enough to see that Thunder's weapon is near enough for me to stretch out and grab it. As I try to do that, I ask if he has his cell on him to get someone from the clubhouse to give us some cover.

I stretch out and grab the gun, dust flies near my arm as I back up, so this bastard is still there waiting for us to come into view.

I look up and see a fork in the tree. If I can get up there, it will give me an advantage as this shooter won't expect that, and I will have a bird's-eye view of where he is.

"Thunder, you okay? Do you think you can give me a leg up to that fork in the tree?" I ask him. "I know you've got a wound in your arm, but if you can, I can maybe pick him off," I state, looking him over.

"Yep, let's do this, Pip, and make your shot count," he responds.

I shove the weapon in my waistband, snug against my spine, lift my leg into Thunder's cupped hands, and use it to spring up and grab the tree where it splits. I manage to scramble up and keep as flat as I can, leaving my legs dangling down.

I'm scanning where I think the bullets came from and hear Thunder talking to someone on his cell. I see a slight movement directly in front of us, behind some thick shrubs, *'got ya,'* I think to myself.

"Torch is on his way, Pip," Thunder tells me while keeping Coal beside him. Coal is positively vibrating, wanting to get out there and hurt someone.

The shooter stands, and I take my shot, *whop*, straight in his shoulder. He cries out and ducks behind the shrubs.

I keep still, keep my aim straight, and my eyes glued to that damn shrub.

"I got him Thunder in his shoulder," I report.

"Keep your eye open, Pip," he responds.

The shooter comes back into view, taking off in the opposite direction. I take another shot and hit him in the leg, which brings him down. I notice another movement and see Torch on the other side of the perimeter fence running to catch up with the shooter. He soon grabs him as I downed him with that last shot.

"Got him Thunder, in his leg, and Torch has grabbed him" I look down from my position to grin at him.

"Pip," I hear shouted and look around from my perched position to see Brand storming towards us.

"Here," I shout to him.

"Where the fuck are you, Pip?" he shouts as he storms around the tree.

Thunder points upwards, and I look downwards with a grin on my face.

"What the hell are you doing up there?" he shouts.

"Shooting a shooter," I blandly respond.

"Get down here," he says with a huff.

"Give me a hand then," I say after shoving the weapon back in my waistband.

Brand catches me as I hang from the tree and steady's me once I am standing again.

I turn to Thunder and step to him and put my arms around his waist and hug him. I have to look around when I hear growling, and it's not Coal.

"Come on, you two, let's get you indoors," Brand states.

"Is Torch okay? Did he keep hold of him?" I ask while giving Thunder a shoulder to lean on.

"Oh, yes, he has him. He'll be in the basement soon," Brand grimly says.

"Basement? No, don't tell me," I say and just keep heading for the clubhouse.

Once indoors, Doc grabs Thunder and takes him off to his medical room, and I call Coal to me as he is still a bit high and alert. I take my time stroking and talking to him in a low soothing tone, to get the tension out of him.

"Brand, I'm going to take Coal to my room, have a shower and calm us both down. I will be back in a while as I need to get the meal finished. Go do what you have to do and don't worry about me. I'm okay, a little frazzled but good," I state.

"Oh no, you're not disappearing. I want to know what the fuck you thought you were doing?" he shouts, which takes me back as I have no idea why he is so pissed off.

"I was doing nothing but having a walk with Thunder until he got shot, and then I protected us both," I shout back with my hands on my hips.

Sniper walks up and puts a leash on Coal, and half drags him off as he's starting to vibrate again.

"You should have stayed down, no place for a woman up a fucking tree shooting at someone trying to kill you both," he shouts again.

"Fuck you, Brand. I will do whatever I need to do to protect myself and my friends," I'm screeching at this point.

"No, you will not. You will do as you're told," he's now nearly nose to nose with me.

"I will not. I will do as I need at the time I need to. You are not my father, brother, or even lover, so you get no say in what I do," which I say in a quiet, controlled voice. I don't even give him time to respond. I storm off up the stairs to my room.

Fifteen minutes later, Sniper knocks, opens the door, and shuffles Coal into the room.

"He's only worried, Pip. He cares about you, and it scared him. Try giving him some leeway for his attitude, babe." he says, looking me straight in the eye.

I just nod and grab Coal when he jumps on the bed with me. I wrap my arms around him and bury my face in his neck. I hear the door close as Sniper leaves. My shoulders start to shake, and I sob into Coal's neck, letting all the fear out.

****BRAND****

I watch as Pip storms up the stairs. I know I was being unreasonable, but I couldn't help myself. The fear just took over. Now I have to think about how I'm going to put that right.

"You want her as an old lady, you got to get your temper under control, she ain't nothing like the bunnies, she's strong, confident, and intelligent, she ain't gonna let you bully her," Crank tells me quietly.

"I know Crank, I was worried, and it all spilled out with fear for her safety," I respond.

He pats my shoulder and wanders back over to his corner of the common room.

I take a deep breath, calm myself, and head to the basement. Now maybe we can find out some answers.

Going down the stairs to the basement, I pass a couple of doors, one room we fitted out as a wine/beer cellar, the other as a general storage room, and I head for the door at the end of the corridor. I don't hear anything as the room has a panel that springs out to reveal the main room. That room has good drainage and is soundproofed, also fully tiled, so it's easy to spray down when needed.

In the middle of the room is Cole Barker, tied to a chair by his wrists and ankles. Jeez, he stinks, and that is before I even get close to him.

"Now, what have we here Torch," I ask while walking around this piece of garbage.

"Seems we caught ourselves a shooter," Torch responds with a grin on his face.

The door opens, and I look over to see Shades, Trigger, and Spider enter the room, all looking pretty pissed, I have to admit. They all have a soft spot for Pip now, so I know they'll want a piece of this shit.

"So, Cole, what have you got to tell us?" I ask, standing directly in front of him. "We can do it the easy or the hard way, I don't care which, but you will tell us everything you know."

"I don't know nuthin," he spits out.

"Oh good, I'm pleased ya don't know nuthin'," taking the piss out of him. "Over to you, Torch," I state and step back to lean on the wall.

Torch grins and steps in front of Cole. "I'll ask you once nicely, what do you know, what can you tell us?" he says.

Cole says nothing and stares Torch down or tries to.

Before you can blink, Torch punches him in the face, and we hear Cole's nose break, blood spurting. He then gives him a good half dozen to his body, finishing with another one to his face, knocking him and the chair back until they are flat on the floor and Cole is knocked out cold.

"Did you have to hit him so hard? I wanted a go at him," Spider states as he grabs one side of the chair, and Shades grabs the other, lifting this piece of shit back into a sitting position.

Trigger walks up with the hose and sprays him down with cold water, waking him pretty quickly.

He now has a broken nose, and an eye closed shut with the force of that last blow. He is groaning and leaning forward to try and stop the pain he has in his torso.

"So, you going to talk now? Or can I have my turn now?" Spider says as he is squatting down in front of this piece of garbage.

"Stop, I will tell you what I know," Cole whispers, and that is what he does.

After leaving the basement, I send Gunner and Shoes down to clear up the mess and make sure this piece of shit doesn't try and escape.

As I'm going back up to the common room, I send a group text for everyone to be in Church in an hour.

CHAPTER 14

****PIP****

Waking from a nap when you were upset prior is no fun. I have a dull headache and feel quite out of it. But looking at my watch, I need to make a move to get the evening meal out on time. I nip into the bathroom, have a quick freshen up, then call Coal and make my way downstairs.

I see Thunder sitting with the other old boys, and I go over and sit next to him and hug him.

"You alright Thunder?" I ask while maintaining my hold on him.

"I'm okay, Pip, tough old guy like me, takes more than a couple of bullets to keep me down," he chuckles, but he keeps his arms around me too. We are taking comfort from each other.

"I need to take Coal out. Do you think I need to get someone to come with me?" I ask him.

"Patch," he hollers across the common room.

"Yeah, what's up Thunder?" Patch responds.

I can see Alice is with Patch, so I try and keep my head down as I don't need her hundred and one questions so she can repeat what I say later. I know that sounds a bit nasty, but she is the worst gossip.

"Will you go out back with Pip while she takes Coal for a quick break?" he asks.

"Sure I will," Patch answers, getting up and waiting for me to make a move.

"Thanks, Thunder," I say and reach up and kiss his cheek.

"Come on, Coal," and take off for the back door to the yard.

"Are you okay, Pip? I can take him without you if you want me to," Patch says.

"No, I'm okay Patch, I have to keep going, and we have Cole in the basement so he cannot shoot me from there," I say with half a smile at him.

We stand and wait for Coal to do his business, I clean up after him, and then we wander back in. I send Coal off to Thunder and the other old boys and head for the kitchen.

I see Brand has appeared now and is sitting at the bar talking to Pink, who is serving tonight. He glances over at me, but I just ignore him and go into the kitchen.

Once Sandy and I have the meal moved to the hatch, I grab a bowl of stew and a warm dinner roll and sit at the kitchen island to eat. I take a couple of bites and can't eat anymore, so I quietly take myself and Coal off to my room, where I lock the door and climb into the shower.

Once showered, I get into bed and, thankfully, in just a couple of minutes, am fast asleep.

****BRAND****

Two hours earlier in Church, we all get settled. Thunder tells us exactly what happened out in the yard. He couldn't praise Pip enough for saving them both and at the same time giving me shitty looks.

"Cole Barker is downstairs in the basement, as you all know. At first, he didn't want to talk, but between us, we persuaded him it was a good idea to spill the beans," I tell everyone.

"Down to bare facts. Stephen Woolcombe is the cousin of Officer Bruce Tailor. Woolcombe hired Tailor because of his Officer status to stay under the radar to kill Pip. Tailor hired Cole Barker to take out Pip, so he didn't get his own hands dirty. He paid him $20,000, which we can see coming out of Tailor's account and going into Barkers. In Woolcombe's financials, as we have said before, we found six accounts, one of those offshore. Woolcombe paid Tailor 1 Mil to remove Pip from the picture, why we are still not sure. We know that Woolcombe is running his own drug house, selling to the cartel, and they are demanding more production in the next few months." I tell them everything I know at this point.

The room bursts with noise as everyone starts talking at once.

"QUIET," I shout.

"I have more information sent to me by June Porter, which shows Woolcombe is doing less in his law practice, but more money is going through the business. From the paper trail, June sent it looks like he is money laundering for the cartel." Ace supplies.

"Christ Ace, is June gonna be safe? Maybe, we should get her the hell out of there before he realizes what she's doing!" Tyre says.

"Actually, I agree, Tyre. I think we need to get her here with us where we can keep her safe until this shit show is over with," I state. "Do you all agree with that?"

The 'ayes' go around the room.

"Dagger, I want you to go fetch her. Don't take no for an answer; get her here no matter what." I say with the tone he has no option.

"No problem, Pres, I'll get it done," he replies confidently.

"One thing that I don't understand is, Woolcombe has stolen all this money. He has it all spread across different accounts and offshore, so why is he still running the drug house and working with the cartel? He has enough money to have paid off his debts, has a healthy bank, and retire or work his practice without anything else?" I look around to see if anyone has any ideas.

"He can't get out now, Pres. Working with the cartel is a one-way street. Once you're in, you're in, and there's no way out. He could make billions but couldn't walk away. He is supplying their drugs and laundering their money, so a double whammy so to speak, he has no way out, apart from the bottom of a river with concrete boots." Trigger clarifies.

"Ace, can you put a file together for this FBI man. Then when he gets here, we can just hand it all over," I ask.

"The last thing, what are we gonna do with Cole Barker?" I grin when I ask. "I think we just keep him and then hand him over to FBI. That will keep our hands clean, keep him alive for them to ask him questions too," I say and look around to see if anyone else has anything to add.

Everyone is just shrugging shoulders or nodding in agreement, so I close the meeting down.

****PIP****

I manage to stay out of Brand's way for three days. I just don't want to talk to him. I won't allow someone to speak to me that way without it being warranted and saving Thunder, and my life was justified. If he doesn't like me being capable with a weapon, then he can kiss my ass.

"Can I speak to you, Pip?" Brand says from behind me.

I didn't realize he had followed me out here with Coal. This surprises me as I am a bit jumpy out here still.

"Are you here to apologize?" I ask him.

"I need to know if you have a date for the FBI man coming?" He asks.

"No, I'll give Larry a call and get Bill Forest's cell number and contact him myself. I need this to be over and done with as it has been over a couple of months since I arrived here, and this all started," I respond.

"Let me know when you have the info, and we can make sure everything we have for him is ready to hand over," he replies.

"Do we know why all this is happening? What Woolcombe is involved in?" I ask him.

"Club business Pip, I cannot tell you," He calmly answers.

"You cannot tell me why someone is trying to kill me, why my parent's business partner wants me out of my share of said business, you know, but you won't tell me?" I blandly say. "Is that right?"

He winces but responds, "I cannot tell you, it's club business," he repeats.

"Okay, well, you shove your club business up your ass, and I hope it keeps you warm at night," I spit out and promptly walk-off, calling Coal as I do so.

I quickly trot up the stairs to my room. Grab my backpack and fill it with the bits I brought with me. I go into the bathroom and get my things and then go to the kitchen taking Coal with me to grab his bits. I take myself out the front and toss everything into my SUV.

As I am getting Coal into the back seat, Brand stomps out, shouting to me.

"What do you want, Brand?" I spit at him.

"Where the hell do you think you're going?" he shouts.

"Away from club business," I state calmly while climbing in the driving seat.

Just as I think I am clear, I am lifted out of the vehicle and thrown over Brand's shoulder. He shouts Coal and stomps back into the clubhouse. Everyone stops what they are doing to watch the drama of the moment, which is us.

He stands me up and crosses his arms over his chest, and has a smirk on his face. That finishes me. I fist my hand and punch him as hard as I can, right in his gut. He expels all the air he was holding in his lungs and gives me a nasty look, to which I give him one back.

"Now, now, come on, you two, stand down," Crank tells us.

If Crank weren't eighty years old and earned my respect, I would tell him where to put his advice. Instead, I lift my chin, call Coal, and stomp back to my room, slamming the door behind me.

An hour later, Brand knocks on my door, asking if he can talk to me. I don't respond. He tries a couple more times. Then I hear him walking away.

I stay in my room until I have to let Coal out and then need to feed him. While he is eating, I make myself a sandwich and keep out of everyone's way. I clean up as I don't want club business to be discussed over my leaving a plate and a dog bowl. Yes, I am feeling bitchy.

As I go through the commons back towards the stairs, Brand steps in front of me.

"Can I speak to you?" he asks.

"Are you apologizing?" I ask with a raised eyebrow.

"Nope," he responds.

"Then no, you can't," and I walk away. I'm sick of men that think they can piss you off, and then they never apologize. They expect us to say sorry, so why not them? I had enough of it and was upset that I thought more of him and hoped once this was all over, we could be something.

Two hours later, I have had time to calm down and think, and I was acting somewhat childish. For that, I now need to apologize to Brand.

I leave Coal in my room and go down to the common room. I ask Sniper, who is at the bar if he has seen Brand. He tells me he thinks he went to his room.

"Maybe it would be best if you left him alone tonight, Pip," he says, but he looks a bit embarrassed too.

I smile at him and wander back to the stairs. I will not behave like that again if it is going to make my friends embarrassed. It's not how I usually behave. I think all this uncertainty and worry is eating at my nerves now.

I reached Brand's room and take a deep breath, knock and wait.

"Just a minute," he shouts out.

Brand opens the door, and the first thing I notice is he has nothing on apart from his jeans which have the button and zip undone. Then I notice movement behind him and see Pink naked on his bed. I take a step back, seeing Pink is giving me an embarrassed and worried look. Looking from her to Brand and back again, I turn and start to walk away. Brand grabs for my arm, but I shake him off and walk double quick time.

I hear him spit "Fuck" before I open my room door and enter, quietly closing the door behind me.

I lock my door, lean my back on it and slide down to sit on the floor. Coal jumps off the bed and sits next to me, putting his head on my shoulder. I look at him, and he licks my face, cleaning the tears that are running down.

I hear muffled talking quite a while later as people walk past my door. Soft knocking on my door and Brand saying he needs to speak to me, but I ignore it, he tries again, but I don't respond.

It is dark out now. The clubhouse music is off. It's time for me to move. I have everything still downstairs somewhere, and I am taking off back to where I belong. Back to my trailer and my business, back to my life, I'll take my chances.

I whisper to Coal to come on, and we take off downstairs. We get to the common room, and I see my things on the end of the bar. No SUV keys, but I dig in my bag and grab the spares.

"Where are you going, Pip?" a voice says.

I turn around and see its Crank. "I'm going home Crank, its time," I respond.

"Odd time of the day to be taking off, don't you think?" he asks me.

"Anytime, is a good time to go home, Crank," I reply.

I grab my Glock and shoulder holster, adjust it onto my shoulder, pick up the rest of my things on the bar. Smile to Crank, which is a bit watery, but I'm struggling to hold my tears back.

"See you around, Crank, take care." I step over to him, put my arms around his middle and hug him. As I step to walk away, a small sob leaves my throat, but I don't stop. I walk out the front door to my SUV.

At the gate, Billy 'The Kid' opens the gate when I tell him he does or I go through it. Once out the gate, I drive home to the trailer. I keep a vigilant eye out as I don't want to be taken by surprise with a damn cop cruiser. That's all I need tonight is coming face to face with Officer Shithead.

Arriving at the restaurant, I park up next to the trailer. Grab our things and call Coal. I notice Shoes is walking around the other side of the parking area. I go into the trailer and have to smile as Shoes has kept it spotless in here. You really wouldn't know he had been staying here.

Grabbing a hot drink, I sit and think about what has happened since I was last in the trailer, seems like ages, but my life feels like it has changed forever.

Knocking at the door, then Shoes calls, "You okay, Pip?"

"I will be Shoes. I will be," I respond.

I open the trailer door. He looks me over carefully. Giving me a small smile and tells me if I need anything, just to ask if it is within his power, he'll do whatever he can for me.

Just that kindness has a few tears tracking down my cheek, which makes him look uncomfortable. So, I swipe it away and ask if he wants a drink.

"I have to stay on patrol, Pip, but I will have a quick one with you if we stand outside so I can still see the lot," he responds.

This is precisely what we do, but instead of standing at the trailer, I walk the perimeter with him. My eyes scan the perimeter and I'm listening for anything out of the ordinary. I can hear an owl hooting in the distance which has me softly smiling, but apart from that the only thing noticeable to me is the stillness of the night.

As daylight starts to break, I take myself off to the trailer, telling Shoes to come for breakfast when he is done with his shift.

CHAPTER 15

****BRAND****

Looking in the mirror, I look at what I think is a total idiot, yeah myself, I am a fucking idiot. I couldn't have ruined my chances any more than I did last night. Drinking too much and then letting myself be lead here was just idiotic. I don't know what I was thinking. I've never been with Pink before this, never shown her any interest, so why did she and I even get together last night.

Somehow, I need to put this right with Pip, and I know it's not going to be easy, but I cannot lose her. I just know she's the one for me, which makes what happened last night a fuck up of epic proportions. The thought I lost her before I even got her runs through my mind.

I cannot get the look on her face out of my mind when I opened the door. Devastation is the only way to describe it. The calmness when she walked off was enough to make the hair on my arms stand on end. She didn't even slam her door.

Firstly, I need to get this issue with Woolcombe put to an end. The FBI Agent may be able to bust this wide open and take them down one way or another.

I need to catch Trigger and see if he will keep his eye on Pip while I check out all the businesses today. I also need to see if Dagger has picked up June. In my office, I have a pile of things needing my attention, so it will be a hell of a busy day.

Taking my hung-over self down for breakfast, I find most of them sitting around with what looks like burnt eggs, but I cannot be sure.

What the fuck happened to breakfast as this is precisely like the shit Keely used to serve us.

"What happened to breakfast?" I comment to no one in particular.

"Pink cannot cook, Pres," Dollar replies while scrapping his fork around his plate with a look of disgust.

"Why is Pink cooking?" I look at him, asking with a raised eyebrow.

"Well, no one else here to do it. Sandy refused and went off to clean bedrooms." Eagle jumps in to provide.

"Where is Pip? Why is she not cooking breakfast!" I ask with what is a nasty feeling curling in my stomach and chest.

"She's not here. Left in the middle of the night. She took everything with her," Crank supplies, giving me one hell of a nasty look too.

"She's gone? Why the hell didn't you stop her?" I shout, my temper starting to take hold.

"Not my place to keep her a prisoner, Pres, and I think she was better off out of here as things developed," he states with a sneer on his face.

"As things developed! What the fuck are you talking about?" I snipe at him.

"Well, her finding you balls deep near enough in a club bunny was enough to send her off, don't you think? We know you had words yesterday, but that was just the heat of the moment with everything that happened. You weren't reasonable either Pres, at the end of the day, it's her life on the line, so she needs to be kept informed, and I can understand why she was pissed." he responds, with an even bigger attitude.

"I know I fucked up," I state, but I will put it right. I tell no one in particular.

"I want to know why Pink was available for you last night when she knows you have never been interested before. After all that went down yesterday, tempers and nerves were frayed, which is to be expected. Pip was gutted that Thunder was hurt because of her. That is how she sees it. She has been fucking amazing around here, picking up the slack when Keely and Cathy were tossed out, making special meals for all the brothers if they requested. Couldn't have been prouder of her," Torch states. He's taken a real liking to Pip, and it shows how much he cares about her.

"Pink, come out here," Spider shouts out.

Pink comes out of the kitchen with egg splatter all over her. How the hell did she get like that?

"What was that all about last night, Pink? I don't believe in coincidence, so how come you wait until Pres has had too much to drink and then draw him to his room? Knowing that he and Pip were going to get together later when all this shit show is over with, she's been good to you, told you she would be happy to help you get through an online college, and you crap on her, what sort of bitch are you?" Torch snaps. "And don't think I won't be checking you out because I fucking will."

Pink turns a deep shade of red, and her eyes are darting around all over the common room. She doesn't know where to look.

"ANSWER ME!" yells Torch, who looks like he's ready to tear her apart.

"Nothing, it was nothing," she starts to cry, but she's still not looking anyone in the eye.

"Pink, if you have anything to tell us, you better tell us now," I calmly ask her.

She just shakes her head and looks at the floor.

"Do what you have to do, Torch," I comment and stand to walk away. Before I reach the corridor to my office, I turn and say, "I'm ashamed of my actions last night, not something I would ever have done to anyone. You all know I don't do bunnies and certainly would not do that to someone I hoped to have a future with. I apologize to you all as your President for my actions," then I turn and walk to my office, closing the door quietly behind me.

****PIP****

Shoes and I have finished breakfast and having a cup of coffee before we both retire to bed for a few hours. He's doing something on his phone as all I can hear is tap, tap, tap.

"What are you doing, Shoes, playing a game?" I ask.

"No, I'm trying to build a bit of money, so I can get out of the shithole I live in and buy a small house," he responds. "I'm money trading on Forbes. You know I mentioned it to you before."

"How much do you trade with?" I ask as I move to the seat next to him to see if I can look at what he is doing.

"Only about $300 at a time, got nothing more than that to spare," he states.

"Have you made much?" I say as I lean over to look at his phone.

"So far, I've made about $13,000," he tells me with a touch of pink on his cheeks. He is so sweet. I like him, and he feels like a brother should.

"Why don't you do more of your profit, so it builds faster?"

"Well, I daren't risk losing it all and having to start again," he says, chuckling.

"What if we have a deal? What if I give you $50,000 and you trade that? Whatever you make, we go 50/50 on, but keep the original intact for you always to trade?" I state, getting a bit excited, I have to admit.

"What?" he whispers.

He's looking at me like I have two heads which makes me laugh. I can't help it he looks so stunned.

"Well, if we do that, you will get your money built quicker, and I get a return too, a win-win, why not. And in the meantime, I have two bedrooms here why not stay here with me, it would mean I have someone with me all the time, and you don't have to go to your shithole, if you lose the money, you lose it, whatever." I suggest.

"I couldn't do that, Pip, and Pres would hit the roof. He would rip my kutte before I even got a day further," he says nervously.

"Well, that doesn't work for me Shoes, he may be your Pres, but this is my property and my trailer. He is nothing to me. I hoped we could be really good friends, I've never had friends apart from Liza, and I hoped I could make friends here. I will understand if you really won't consider it," I reply but am deflated and sad that things are not going to be as I had hoped when I came here.

"Let me talk to Trigger and see if he thinks I could without causing myself issues, even if I have to speak to Brand. At the end of the day, I agree, if I do what I'm told, when I'm told, then it shouldn't cause an issue."

"Well, stay for today as we're both tired with being up all night. Were you in the main bedroom or the spare?"

"I stayed in the spare. No way would I take your bed, Pip."

"Great, I'm going to give Coal a quick trip outside then hit the hay for a while," I state and giving a yawn. Boy, I'm tired.

Four hours later, I'm awake listening to the sounds of men talking, banging, a truck in and out. What is the point of trying to sleep any longer? I roll over and see Coal on his bed in the corner, upside down, showing all he has to the world, men, I think to myself.

I jump into the shower, get myself dressed, and grab my dirty clothes. Time to do some domestic duties, I think.

After spending the next hour sorting laundry, tidying up, and then finalizing my list for the restaurant cabinet items, I grab my laptop and test it to see if I have internet access yet.

Wow, I do. Spider and Ace must have set me up without letting me know. This is great. It will save me messing about with messengers now.

I spend the next two hours online shopping. One order for groceries for myself and Shoes in the trailer, one from the list I made for the restaurant, and one for a laptop as a gift.

I finish the chores I wanted to do and hang my washing in the utility, hoping it doesn't embarrass Shoes.

Grabbing my notepad and pen, I leave the trailer as quietly as possible, telling Coal to go lay down and be quiet.

I make my way over to the restaurant's back door, and as I enter the kitchen, I stand still and take it all in. The walls are fully tiled for ease of keeping clean, sinks, dishwashers, food mixers, ovens, fryers, hot plates, fridges, shelving from ceiling to floor, it's impressive and more than I had imagined it would be finished.

As I am standing, taking it all in, someone puts their arm around my shoulders, and as I look up, it's Cali; he is always smiling at me.

"This is amazing, Cali. It's perfect, more than I imagined it would be," I said with a tear that escapes down my cheek.

"So pleased you're happy with it Pip, it was worth all that work to see your face this second in time," he says while using his thumb to wipe the tear away.

"I ordered a huge online shop for the pantry this morning, and once I know the open date, I can get the perishables ordered and delivered," smiling up at him as I say it.

"Come on, let me show you the front," and he places his hand on my back and guides me through the kitchen to the main restaurant area.

Behind the main counter is everything that I will need, organized, unpacked, and ready to use when we open the restaurant. Rows of glassware, cups, saucers, cutlery, napkin holders, and that's without the coffee machines, cold drink dispensers, and the rest.

In the front, as you come into the restaurant from outdoors, on the left is the main restaurant, where tables with fancy tablecloths and center displays will be. On the right is the day restaurant, where the booths are along with the main window and seats in front of the serving counter.

It is perfect, just as I had described to Shades when I gave him all my ideas right at the beginning. Who would have thought the time had flown by to get all this finished.

Amazing, truly, exactly as I had asked for Cali. Just perfect," giving him a beaming smile.

"Okay, you want to come upstairs to see the apartment? Not done, of course, but you can see where we are at," he asks.

"Yes, I do want to see, thank you," following him through the kitchen, outside, and to the staircase on the side of the building.

When we get upstairs, and I see it has been stripped to bare bones, I know they have been working their butts off. I look around and see Red, Nash, Whisky, and Ice hauling all the debris to a shoot they have set up that takes all the rubbish to the dumpster downstairs. They are all covered in so much dust it's a wonder I can tell who is who.

I don't see Shades anywhere, so presumably, he has other things to do now. "Shades not about Cali? I wanted to speak to him about having the staircase outside covered with a door that locks on the bottom, hence, making it safer for Liza when she moves in. And I need to ask him about the extension onto the back for the catering business and a good size office."

He looks at me as though he knows nothing about this, but I am sure I mentioned an extension to Shades.

"I don't know about this, Pip. I will speak to him about it and get him to talk to you as it'll need planning. Do you want it a single story?"

"No, I was thinking of having it two-story so that it could make a second apartment," scrunching my nose up as I don't know what the heck idea I even have in my head at the moment.

"We'll have to put it to Shades as we'll need planning to get it all done."

I wave to everyone and saunter back downstairs, giving another thanks to Cali and taking myself back to my trailer.

Once I open the trailer door, Coal greets me as always, and I let him out to do his business. I sit on the step, watching him while my head is going over everything I have just seen.

Out of the corner of my eye, I notice the cop cruiser going past at a crawling pace. I shout Coal and make my way indoors because now I know how crooked Tailor is. I don't want to have any contact with him at all.

As I go into the trailer, I see Shoes making a fresh pot of coffee, so I give him a thumbs up that I will have one.

"Shoes, that Tailor just crawled past in his cruiser, so I think we need to be alert. He's not given up on whatever he has planned," I state while heading for my bedroom.

When I come back, I have my Glock and all my cleaning gear, unlocking the magazine, sliding the barrel and recoil spring, slide and frame, cleaning and lubricating it all as needed. I place the brush and lubricant back in the cleaning bag and take it back to the bedroom. While there, I decided to wear my custom-made holster that fits my belt. Then I reassemble it, so it is ready for use.

I load the Glock and place it in the holster. Now I feel more confident. Seeing him ride past has rattled my nerves, but now I am ready for the rest of the day.

CHAPTER 16

*****PIP*****

The morning is glorious for this time of the year. It won't be long before Thanksgiving. That would be a great time to open the restaurant and do a promo, so the 50th customer to order gets their meal free. I need to think about a manager that can deal with all this type of thing.

Once I have let Coal out, fed him, and myself, I notice that Shoes has already gone to bed which suits me as I don't want him to overhear the conversations I will be having in a short while. I have a secret smile on my face with the idea I have hatched and will now implement.

Checking the time, I see that Larry should be in his office, and I could catch him before he makes a start on his day. Grabbing my cell and my notepad, I settle on the bench seat and make my call.

"Morning Larry, do you have a few minutes to chat with me" I quickly ask as Larry picks up my call.

"I can spare you about ten minutes, Pip."

And I quickly lay out my plan and tell him to sort it as soon as he can. He gives me Bill Forest's number too so I can arrange a meet-up with him.

I feel rather smug with myself at the moment and hope my plans play out the way I want them to.

I grab a cold drink, then settle back for my next call.

"Good morning." I inquire as my call is picked up. "Am I speaking to Bill Forest?"

"Speaking," the man responds.

"My name is Piper East, and Larry Thomas gave me your number."

"Fabulous, I was going to contact you tomorrow. Are you alright?" he asks, sounding somewhat concerned, I have to admit.

"I'm back at my trailer now. The restaurant is finished but not open yet. The company I used has and is doing a fantastic job, not hanging around either."

"Give me your address, and I'll see you after lunch tomorrow. We can get together with the MC that is helping you and get everything in one place so we can see exactly what is going on and what viable evidence we have for me to work with."

"I will give you the clubhouse address as everything that has been collected is there for you to pick up. You can also ask them the questions you have that way."

Not sure I want to go back to the clubhouse, but I suppose I don't have a choice if I want to know what the hell is going on myself. But it will be nice to see the old boys. I love them to bits and miss them chatting and ribbing me, even their requests for meals or cakes.

Rinsing out my cup and putting my notepad safely away in my bedroom, I make my way out of the trailer to see if Shades is on-site this morning. I leave Coal inside as I don't want him running up and down the stairs to the apartment where they are all working.

Entering the apartment, I notice a little boy playing in a corner, sitting on a rug with a few toys. Shades is working on a table next to him.

Wandering over, the little boy looks up, and I wave at him. He waves back with the most gorgeous smile, obviously not shy.

Shades looks to see who the boy is waving at and sees me walking over. He keeps an eye on the child all the time.

"Oh my, you are a handsome little man," I say as I reach them.

"My son Tyler," Shades tells me, looking a bit worried.

"Is he okay? Why have you got him here at work?" asking as I kneel with the little boy and start playing with his toy truck, to which he giggles and joins in.

"Babs came by and dumped him in the door. She just damn took off without a backward glance," he tells me, looking pissed off about it too.

"Well, I don't think it's safe for him in here Shades, how about I take him with me to the trailer, and I'll watch him while you work?"

"I couldn't ask you to do that, Pip."

"You're not asking. I'm offering," I respond while tickling this little fella. He's laughing and wriggling as I play with him.

"I would be grateful, Pip. I'm working on the plans for the extension, I need to make sure you have the office, and the catering rooms set out as you need them. I also hear you want another apartment too," giving me an exasperated look at the same time.

"Well, yes, I do. But if you don't want to take that work on, I can find another company, Shades," I state, knowing it will piss him off.

"You won't get another company. We can do all the work that you need. But the more you add, the longer it will take to get it all finished."

"I know that, and I'm not worried. I'm going to speak to Dollar as I want to give him a large sum so you will have the finances to get whatever you need without having me sign off anything," knowing this will give him a bit of relief from worrying if they have enough money to continue on with. How affluent the club finances are, I have no idea.

"Come on, little man," picking up Tyler and a couple of his toys. "Has he eaten Shades?" I ask as I start to walk off.

"He had breakfast Pip, but he may need some lunch now," he responds, looking sheepish.

I nod and carry on down the stairs and back to the trailer. Feeding Tyler and spending time with him is great fun. He's a cheerful little man, and after he has his fill, I can see his eyes starting to close. I place him in my bed and sit next to him. Within a couple of minutes, he's fast asleep. Smiling, I leave the door open slightly and go clean up our mess.

Picking up my cell, I give Dollar a ring. We chat for a few minutes about the work done and what I still need doing. I tell him to provide me with the club bank details again to transfer half a million into that account. I organized that with my bank and then rang him back to let him know it's done. He confirms the money has been transferred.

The next call is to Eagle as secretary of the club. I hope he will know who I can contact about the advertising for staff, starting with a manager as I need someone to throw ideas at and get things done when I need it.

Eagle is great. He organizes the advertisement and tells me I don't have to pay as he will put the ad up in the local bookstore as they have a notice board where people can check regularly. One of the good things about living in a small town, I would think.

"Pip, you want a drink?" Shoes asks me as he comes out of his bedroom.

"Yes, please, I'm going to check on Tyler too."

"You got Shades, son, here?" he looks pretty surprised at me.

"Yeah, apparently his mother dumped him and drove off this morning, leaving Shades in a tough spot. He had him in the apartment upstairs when I went to check in, and I told him I would have him here, far safer to be here with me."

"She's a nasty piece of work, known all over town as a piece of ass, and most people feel sorry for Shades having to deal with her. But he loves his son". Shoes supplies this tidbit of information.

"Is she into something she shouldn't be?"

"I would not be surprised. Her mother was just like her. They live in the rough part of the town," he has his nose curled, which makes me giggle as he is living there too, but he thinks less of them for it.

Going into the bedroom, I see Coal lying next to Tyler, who has his arms around his neck and kissing his face. Coal is just letting him do it. I chuckle to myself as my boy is such a good boy.

I pick up Tyler and take him into the bathroom. After a bit of a fuss, I manage to get him sorted out, and we go back into the kitchen area, where I get him a drink of milk. He's such a lovely child, easy to look after.

Knocking at the trailer door grabs my attention. Shoes answers, and its Shades checking if all is good with Tyler.

I bring Shades up to date with how good Tyler has been, that he has had a nap, had a snack before that, and just finished some milk. I offer to have him anytime as he was a delight to have around.

Shades is grateful, but he looks worried about putting me out, but I put his mind at rest and tell him I love kids and wish I had had siblings. So anytime, I would be more than happy to have him.

After Tyler and Shades have gone, I put a quick casserole in and tell Shoes I need to update Brand on Bill Forest coming tomorrow to meet them all. I'm not looking forward to this call, but it has to be made.

Shoes gives me a look to say it'll be okay, but I don't feel very confident about that.

****BRAND****

I am sitting in my office looking over all the evidence we have regarding Woolcombe, Tailor, and Barker, it's all tying up well.

Dagger has returned with June, who has a lot of evidence for us to wade through, statements, emails, video evidence of meetings in his office, and even taped phone conversations. June has been busy.

She is much younger than I thought she was going to be. I had it in my mind she was thirty or more with being secretary for Pip's parents, but it seems she was only with them nine months before they died. She is only twenty-one and feisty. I have to smile when I see the attitude she is throwing at Dagger. It reminds me of Pip. I have to admit.

My cell rings, and I pick it up to check who's ringing as I cannot be bothered with any more trouble just now.

When I see its Pip, my heart takes a leap, and I quickly accept the call.

"Hello, Pip," I quickly say.

"Hello Brand, I just wanted to let you know that Bill Forest will be here tomorrow afternoon, and he's coming straight to the clubhouse. As soon as he arrives, would you be kind enough to let me know, and I'll get Shoes to bring me over for the meeting. If you don't want me at the meeting, please send him to me as soon as you have finished. Thank you."

Before I get the chance to respond, she turns off the call. I sit looking at my cell, thinking, awe fuck, she still is not willing to talk to me.

But I collect all the evidence we have and search for Spider and Ace to get this all set up in Church ready for tomorrow. I also want them to put a new security lock on the Church door as I feel Pink is up to more than just causing a hassle with Pip and me.

Speaking to Spider, I make sure he is up-to-date with everything I know and that I want him to set it up as a timeline if he can, so when Forest adds his evidence, it may slip in and show us the gaps we have.

As I head back to my office, Torch catches me.

"Can I have a minute, Pres?"

"Sure, why not" I respond, rubbing my neck as I feel more trouble is brewing.

"I checked out Pink as I had this gut feeling something was going on. She had a staggering $10,000 added to her bank account a week ago. I saw it's from Keely, and I know that because Ace has checked the account number against our records for wage payouts. So why is Keely paying Pink that amount of money to wreck your relationship with Pip?   AND, Keely had $30,000 paid into her account ten days ago by Officer Bruce Tailor. It seems all these bitches are out to bring Pip down." He's growling and snapping out all this information.

"Well, tomorrow Bill Forest will be here. Make sure this information is in the file and on the timeline set up in Church. Make sure you lock the Church door. You need to get the key from Spider. I had him put a new security lock on as I was uneasy about Pink."

"Fucking hell Pres, this is such a crock of shit. Pip has been kind to everyone, and look how she has been repaid. Will she be here tomorrow for the meeting? If so, at least she will hear all the bull that Pink pulled and may forgive you". He says the last with a bit of smirk, but I'm not holding my breath.

Before we can say anything else, Chip rushes into the office.

"Pres, I just double-checked Woolcombe's financials for the day, and he just transferred half a million to an unknown offshore account. Ace is double-checking as he has a nasty feeling about something," he gushes before he even takes a second breath.

"Christ, it just gets worse and worse," I respond. "Tell Ace to update me as soon as he has more info."

"No need, Pres, I got it, the account is to a Peter Graves, he is known as Ghost, he's a hitman." Ace informs me.

"We need to get Pip back here ASAP," but I know she is not coming if I ask her. "You need to go Ace or send Spider. Either of you will have more success than I will. Oh, and get Pink in the fucking basement too". This earns me shocked looks, but I don't care. I'm past playing with these vindictive bitches.

****PIP****

Spider rides into the parking lot at the restaurant and parks next to my trailer. He straddles his bike and removes his helmet.

I open the trailer door and give him a questioning look before turning around and disappearing back where I came from.

Hanging his helmet on his handlebars, he throws his leg over his bike seat and walks to the trailer. Taking a deep breath, he steps in and closes the door behind him.

"Hi, Pip. Got news I need to talk to you about."

"Do you want a drink Spider, hot or cold? I have both," I ask.

"No thanks, babe. Can we sit?"

After grabbing a cold juice, I sit at the dining table and wait for what he has to say.

Shoes appears from the bedroom, grabs a drink, and leans against a cupboard in the kitchen area, showing no sign of leaving, so Spider decides to continue anyway as Shoes is on patrol and keeping Pip safe.

"We have, as I said, this is new information. Officer Tailor paid Keely $30,000, who paid Pink $10,000 to sleep with Pres by any means necessary. You two having words together was her perfect time as she plied him with drinks until drunk out of his head, which none of us have ever seen. He has also never slept with a bunny, ever, so it took all of us by surprise when this happened, and believe me, we have all made his life miserable over it too. But regardless, we also found that Woolcombe has paid half a million to someone called Peter Graves, aka Ghost who is a hitman." Spider pauses with a look I don't even recognize.

"What the fuck!" Shoes growls from the kitchen area.

"With that in mind, Pip, we want you to come back to the clubhouse as it will be safer for you than here at this time. We will give the FBI agent all the info tomorrow, and he will have more resources than us, but we can at least keep you within the brick walls, which will keep you safe," Spider states.

"No, I'm not going back to the clubhouse to stay. I will come tomorrow for the meeting, but I will not be staying. If you push this, I won't even come to the meeting. I will get in touch with Bill Forest and ask for a contact for some muscle to help with patrolling the area, including my property out the back," I respond flatly, with no emotion whatsoever.

"Pip, it may be something you need to think about. I know you don't want to, and I know why but it is about keeping you alive," Shoes responds, coming to sit next to me.

"I can't Shoes, and I don't want to. I'm tired of having shit happen to me. I need to take my life back, and if that means I die doing it my way, then so be it."

"I can't persuade you, can I?" Shoes asks.

"No, this is my stand, and you won't make me change my mind. What you can do is get me a shotgun. I know how to use one. I have my Glock, but to have an extra would not hurt," I state, looking from one to the other.

"Okay, Pip, I'm with you, no matter what, I will stand or go down with you," Shoes states and grabs my hand and squeezes it.

After Spider tries to convince me otherwise, he eventually gives up. Shoes tells Spider to keep a close eye on the cameras, and any movement, let him know so we can weapon up quickly. After that,

Spider takes off. As soon as he leaves, I double-check all the trailer windows are now closed and locked and close all the shades. The less someone can see in, the better.

Shoes takes Coal out for a quick walk to his area. And that is how we batten down the hatches for the night, although it is still early.

CHAPTER 17

****PIP****

Thankfully nothing untoward occurred overnight. We were both on tenterhooks waiting for something to kick off and didn't even think to go to bed. We chatted, and I threw an idea at Shoes, to which he was happy to help me plan if he could. I laid it all out to him, and he had this smirk that I had not seen before, but it made me point at him and laugh.

We talked about what had happened with Brand, and he saw my point of view but could understand that forcing a split between myself and the Pres made me come out of the clubhouse and, by doing so, left me vulnerable once more.

He was also majorly pissed with Pink for all the hurt she had caused and for a relatively small amount of money as she would lose a lot more than that when she was thrown out of the club as she would lose her home too.

Together we got some breakfast thrown together and ate quietly. Shoes took Coal out while I cleaned up, and I heard the men turning up for work. I stayed in the trailer out of the way.

Shades came over and knocked, giving a shout-out who it was. I shouted back for him to come in.

"Hiya Pip. Any idea what time the agent is coming?"

"No, he just said after lunch. I told Brand to give me a call when he arrives, and I will come over," I tell him while trying to keep busy doing some wiping around in the kitchen area.

"Oh, okay, I'll come over and ride in the SUV with you."

"No need, Shoes said he would come over with me. It was his night off last night and tonight. We didn't sleep at all last night with all the worry, but we will tonight, I'm sure."

"I'll go over with you anyway if that's alright. I'm here working, so can go and come back at the same time" he's looking closely at me, looking for a reaction, I'm sure.

"Are the other four here today too?" meaning Whisky, Ice, Nash, and Cali.

"Yes, we are putting in new wiring today. It was pretty messed up."

"Alright, Shades, I'll give you a shout before we go over to the clubhouse," I'm happy to travel with him and Shoes.

"Oh, did you know June is here?" he informs me.

"No, will I see her at the clubhouse?"

"I'm sure you will hear her rather than see her. She's giving Dagger some attitude," he says, laughing. "She whacked him over the head, so he threw her over his shoulder and then packed her in the van to bring her here," he is snickering now.

"Oh my god, I wish I had seen that," I laugh myself. I only met June twice, but I liked her, and the second time I met her, she slipped that note in my hand.

"All fun at the clubhouse for you all then."

"We all miss you for sure, and your damn fine cooking."

I don't respond to that and just find something else to keep me looking busy until he returns to work.

"I'm gonna head out, Pip. Stay indoors until I come back. I will only be gone about an hour. Coal doesn't need to go out as he went about fifteen minutes ago," Shoes tells me as he is grabbing his kutte and boots.

I give him a thumbs up and take myself off to my bedroom. I tidy up and then grab my laptop.

Back in the dining area, I sit with a cold drink and fire up my laptop. I need to check out the kitchen units and other items necessary for the apartment. I know Liza will only come with her clothes and bits, so I'll need to furnish it all out so she can just move in.

Shades had given me a website address to check on what I want for the kitchen, bathroom, and utility, and all I need to do is jot down which I want him to go with. After I have that organized, I check out places for furniture and have another list ready for when the apartment needs finishing. I can't wait for her to get here. It will be great to have her around again.

The door opens sharply, making me jump, and Shoes comes in with an excited look on his face.

"What? What is it?" I ask him, not knowing if I should be panicking or not.

He gives me that evil grin and chuckles and then burst out laughing, hands on his knees as he tries to get himself under control.

"What, tell me."

"Pip, you would never guess in a million years what I just found out thanks to your plan," still chuckling.

"Keely is the bastard daughter of, you guessed it, Officer Bruce Tailor. She is therefore related to Woolcombe. She also has a drug debt she couldn't pay, but the kicker is, and I found this out from Cathy, who is out of here today I have to tell you, that Keely was planted here at the club, so Tailor knew what was going on and when so a fucking mole."

"Oh my god, you have to tell Brand when we get to the meeting. I know he told me Prospects could not go to Church, but you will be, I'll make sure of it." I stick my chin out with my determined and stubborn head-on.

"Your plan of catching Cathy and giving a few threats worked great. She sang like a fucking bird," Shoes says, still laughing.

We keep discussing what he found out while we had a quick lunch. Shoes takes Coal out, so we know he will be okay while we are at the clubhouse. Then we are all ready for the call letting us know Bill Forest has arrived.

Shades knocks on the trailer and shouts, time to go as he just had the call from Spider to say they are ready for us. I give my SUV keys to Shoes which makes him grin, and I climb in the back, fastening my seat belt and holding onto my notepad, folder, and purse.

When we arrive at the clubhouse, we are ushered into Church quickly. Shoes is told to wait outside, but I insist he has to come in as he has vital information he just found out. So, Brand allows it, although he doesn't look too happy about it either.

I see they have an entire wall of corkboard set up with a timeline pinned with notes. Not wanting to get too involved with that, I find an empty seat next to Bomber, and Shoes sits next to me on the other side.

Bill Forest is introduced, and the meeting gets underway. Spider starts to run through what we have so far. I hold my hand up, and everyone looks at me with a grin as I must look like I am in school. I explain that Shoes has extra information, and he stands and informs them of the connection between Tailor and Keely and that

Cathy had nothing to do with any of it, and she was on her way out of state as we speak.

Bill Forest then updates us on what he found.

"I'm sorry, Pip, but we have the evidence that Woolcombe had your parent's accident orchestrated. He wanted them out of the business as they found out through the financials that he was laundering money for the cartel. The work, your parents, were doing was all legit legal work. They were clean," he takes a breath and continues, "We also know he used someone called Peter Graves, aka Ghost, for the job."

With that, Trigger jumps up, cursing. He points at the timeline to show Forest that a hit had been put out on me from Woolcombe to Graves, and they have the proof from Woolcombes' financials."

"But why does he want me dead? I still don't see why, even with all we have collected, all that evidence, and still none of it makes sense as to why he wants me dead," I state, getting more than a bit stressed at this point.

"I think you have something that he needs, something your parents have left you," Forest tells me while looking at me intensely.

"I have nothing. They didn't leave me anything about Woolcombe!"

"Did you collect everything from Larry when he read you the will? Have you opened everything he gave you?" this was Dollar chipping in.

"I have a sealed folder that Larry gave me, and I can tell my father wrote the message on it which just says *'Love you Pip, always have, always will, Dad,'* and that is all it says!" I have a tear running down my cheek. "I haven't opened it as yet because it would open the flood gates of despair at losing them, and I didn't want to do that, they wouldn't want me to do that, so I was waiting until I felt comfortable enough to open it," I state.

"Is the envelope safe?" Forest asks.

"Yes, it's in the trailer. I nearly brought it with me for some reason and then changed my mind."

"Could someone get it and bring it here?" Brand questions.

"I suppose so. Coal will let Cali in. I'm sure as he knows him now. Cali sometimes sits and has a cold drink with me at lunchtime if I'm running Coal at that time, so I know he'll have no issue with letting Cali in the trailer."

"Alright, give Cali a ring and tell him where to get the folder, and while we wait, we can grab a drink ourselves." Brand supplies.

So that is what I do. I give Cali the instructions of where I put the folder and told him to make sure Coal was left in the trailer and to please bring the folder to me. I suppose it is good that Cali, Whisky, Nash, and Ice were left to work on the wiring while this meeting was being held.

While we are in the commons, I go to the old boys and give them all a hug and kiss on their cheeks. I miss them all so much. They just mean so much to me already.

Making my way over to grab a drink, Brand asks to speak to me. I cannot avoid him forever, so I say yes, and he leads me to his office, closing the door quietly behind him.

"I need to explain what happened, Pip, and apologize for my behavior," he takes a deep breath, but I stop him before he says anymore.

"Nothing to apologize for, Brand. We are not an item. We weren't an item at that time, so what you do is none of my business."

"You know I want to get to know you, Pip, that I want to make a life with you eventually."

"No, don't say more. I don't want to hear it. I have so much happening in my life that I can't handle any of this. I have to stay alive at this point, and a relationship is the last thing I need now. I think we should just stay as friends and not cause upset for the club," I state, while my heart is beating way too fast, and it hurts to say this, but it's the truth as I see it now.

"If that is what you want, then I am happy for us to not be at loggerheads with each other. I don't like that you are not speaking to me and avoiding me at all costs."

"Friends," I state while holding my hand out.

"Friends," he responds and holds my hand.

We go back to the commons and see Cali arrive. He has the folder in his hand and walks over to me.

"All was okay at the trailer Pip, Coal let me in with no problem, and I let him have a quickie, then put him back in," he states while he hands me the folder.

Now we have the folder, we all go back into Church. I'm sitting staring at the sealed folder, one of my dad's tricks, seal everything. I take a few deep breaths and then break the seal and open it.

The first thing on top of the folder is a letter.

My Dearest Pip,

If you are reading this, then your mom and I are no longer with you. We want you to know that we so love you and will be looking down on you from where we are. We are giving you this folder as it could be the difference between you living and being murdered. Yes, we have been murdered. However, the way we have died, it was not an accident.

You will find statements, photographs, and evidence to back up all I am telling you. You will need to give all this to the FBI. Our partner Stephen Woolcombe as you will see from the proof, has a drug house where he supplies the cartel, but he also provides the cartel with women. He's into human trafficking.

This is why we have been murdered. We have proof that he is supplying women. He has a string of men who snatches women off the street to order. You will see a page from his order book in the file. These horrendously evil men order what color hair, size, the age they want a woman to be, and then Stephen has these women abducted to fill the order.

You will see a key taped at the back of the file. It's in my safe deposit box. All the information you need is with it so you can get the box. In the box is the rest of the evidence. I have only given you a snippet in this folder. Do not go to the safe deposit box on your own. Your security has to be the best, or he will have you murdered too. If you're dead, no one will find out what you know, and he is home free.

Stay safe, be wise, don't be impulsive, and don't be stubborn. Live a long and happy life, Pip. We didn't want to leave you, and we wish we had had more children so you had a sibling, but it was not to be.

We love you forever, and an extra day.

Dad & Mom xxxx

I hand the letter and folder to Shoes, who was sitting next to me, and I walk out of the room as I cannot cope with anyone looking at me right now.

I sit at the bar with my head in my hands and sob. A heavy gut-churning sobbing that I cannot stop. When I feel a pair of arms coming around me to hug me to them, I realize it's Brand. He just holds me while I let it all out.

Once I have myself nearly under control, I lift my face and say thank you for being there for me. He just gives me that half-smile that makes his dimple pop.

We go back to Church, where everyone is going over the folder contents and placing notes on the timeline board.

Bill Forest comes over to me and asks if we can get the safe deposit box tomorrow as it is too late in the day to travel to Nebraska for it today.

I agree we would go first thing and walk over to Shoes to see if he is ready to leave, giving Shades the heads up.

We say our farewells and head out.

CHAPTER 18

****PIP****

Morning came around far too quickly, and although I had not slept the night before, I only napped on and off as my mind was too full of all that we had talked about. I know Shoes didn't sleep well as he got up two or three times during the night, and I had to smile as he was trying so hard to stay quiet.

Showering and dressing quickly, I grab just a piece of toast off Shoes plate as I sit at the dining table. He gives me a smile and a shake of his head.

"You okay, Pip?" he gives me a straight look, showing he is worried.

"I'm going to be when all this is over with. Are you staying here? I need to know Coal will be alright," before he can respond, I continue, "Shoes, if anything should happen to me, will you keep Coal, make sure he's loved and looked after?"

"Nothing is going to happen to you, Pip."

"I need to know he'll be alright. I want him to be with you," I persist.

"Alright, I promise, but nothing is going to happen to you. You only just came into my life, and I don't want to lose you. You're like the sister I never had," he states with a hitch in his breath.

He cannot know how much that means to me, especially with what I have in motion now. I will need to speak to Larry when I get back, and Bill Forest has gone.

Knocking on the door takes me by surprise, and Shoes checks who it is before he opens it.

"Ya ready, Pip?" Brand asks as he enters the trailer.

"Yes, let me grab my purse."

I make sure I have the key and information for the bank and turn to Shoes and put my arms around him and hug him. I don't look into his face, or I will burst into tears. I scratch Coal behind his ears and tell him to stay with Shoes. Then step out of the trailer.

This will be a long journey, and we may not get to the bank today unless the roads are good to us.

As I climb into the SUV, Bill Forest turns to me.

"Morning Pip."

"Morning, I hope everyone is ready for the trip," I say with a wry twist to my smile.

"Oh, we're going to the airport Pip, I have a flight booked for us all, we are flying to Nebraska, and I have agents waiting to pick us up at that end and take us to get the safe deposit box. Then we can get you all back here today." Forest supplies.

I look around, astonished at everyone in the vehicle. Brand smiles and looks pretty laid back about it. Trigger, Patch and Torch look far more uptight.

We arrive in Nebraska and are hustled into a black Chevrolet Tahoe with blacked-out windows. Before I can take a second breath, we are off to get the safe deposit box.

Upon arriving at the bank, I am surrounded by the four MC men and six FBI Agents. Talk about overkill, I think to myself. We enter the building and go to inquiries, but before I can say anything, Forest states we have an appointment with the manager to open a safe deposit box.

He earned himself a nasty look for that jerk of a move. I am capable of speaking. He lifts one eyebrow when he sees me giving him evil looks.

The manager arrives, and I hand over the information my dad left me, which is permission for me to have the box opened on his demise, and I have his death certificate as proof.

We are taken to a room, and I insist only Forest and Brand come with me, everyone else to stay where they are.

The room is not very big but enough for us at the table to see without being on top of each other. The manager brings the box, and we open it with the keys we each have. I don't open the box until he has left the room.

I look over at Brand and Forest and take a breath, then lift the lid. It is crammed full of papers, photographs, and a journal.

The photographs make me want to be sick. Images of women tied up and have clearly been beaten. Underweight and abused. Each picture has information on the back. The journal shows names, dates, places, and amounts paid. It's making me gag thinking of these poor women being abducted and put through this.

Everything in the box proves that Woolcombe supplies drugs and women to the cartel, even names of the cartel members involved, everything that the FBI needs to bring them down. But will it get the women back from where they were sold?

"Pip, this is massive. We need to keep you safe until we have everyone rounded up. I want to put you in WITSEC," Forest states.

"No, absolutely not. I'm not going into WITSEC, and if you try and make me, I will go to the nearest newspaper and spill my guts on the whole thing. Don't think I'm joking. I'm deadly serious," I respond and glare at him as I say it.

"We'll make sure she stays safe," Brand jumps in. "We can have roving patrols at the business, or Pip can come back to the clubhouse. You can provide extra bodyguards if needed, Forest. You have the information you want. Pip has done everything you've asked. Now it's time to do your bit."

****BRAND****

I can see Pip has had about enough. She's tiring fast. This is such an enormous roller coaster of emotion. Finding all those photographs was horrendous; they made your gut turn.

Forest arranges the flight home, and we get back just before everyone at the clubhouse would turn in for the night, but I take Pip back to the trailer as she is worried about Coal.

I was going to drop off Trigger and Torch at the clubhouse, but they want to stay with Pip until she is safely home. They arrange the extra security on the premises to be in place before we arrive.

Arriving at the trailer, Shoes opens the back door and helps Pip out. Coal is jumping about and barking with excitement, and I see Chip and Mallet on opposite sides of the area. They both just give an acknowledgment by tipping their head and then turn back to looking away from the parking area.

Entering the trailer, Shoes makes everyone a drink, and Pip fills him in on what we found. He looks horrified, but also you can see how angry he is too.

"Don't wander about on the property, Pip, until this is all nailed down, don't make yourself an easy target," I explain how we're going to have the gym closed down so the three from that business can help as extra security. They are all trained with weapons, so we have no issue with that; we all have concealed carry permits.

I start to laugh, and with the looks I'm getting, I have to explain. "Well, Pip, it seems that Glide, Thunder, and Sniper have decided to come out of retirement, and they are also going to go on security duty. It's a damn good job they all attend the gym four times a week," I state. "Oh, and Crank is going to sit in here with you while they do it," and with that, I start with a belly laugh imagining Pip having to put up with him for hours on end.

"What the!" Pip responds, looking aghast.

"Well, it was them coming to you or you going to them at the clubhouse, no options but those, so they decided to come to the mountain, which is you."

"Right, we are going to need to get some shuteye, and Molly will be giving Trigger some bother about being late home," I snicker, much to Trigger's distaste.

Shoes let us out, and I hear him lock the trailer door before we even get into the vehicle. He's turning out to be protective of Pip. You can see the genuine caring between them both. It makes me jealous as shit, but nothing I can do about it, or it would cause even more of a rift between myself and Pip.

Once we arrive back at the clubhouse, everyone asks what happened, what is going on, and I decide we will have a meeting as it will be easier. I look around and see Pink standing behind the bar.

"Take her to the basement and put her in lock up," I say to Torch quietly.

"Oh yes, now you're talking," he says with a nasty smile on his face.

Once he has her locked up, I go behind the bar and grab myself a beer. I then tap on the bar top and get everyone's attention. Between us, Torch, Trigger, and I update everyone on what we found.

Crank is vibrating with fury. He lost a daughter years ago when she just up and disappeared. A few years later, they found her body, she had been abused badly, and she had thick scarring on her wrists and ankles where she had been chained. Crank has every reason to hate these people, and it explains why he loves Pip so much. He sees her as a daughter, I am pleased he is a healthy shit as he will hopefully have a few years with her, but being eighty, I know he takes it one day at a time.

June appears from the corridor, and I don't know if she heard any of the meeting or not, but I would think not from how she is acting. She comes over and asks me if everything is alright. I tell her a quick update, to which she is shocked as she had no evidence of trafficking, but she said he was such a piece of shit it should not surprise her.

June also surprised me when she said she has a carry permit as her father was an ex-marine, and he taught her how to shoot. She has a sniper rifle and knows how to use it. Offering to be wherever I may need her if there was a gap in security.

Hearing this, Dagger throws his teddy bear in the corner, which makes me smile as they once again go off arguing like a pair of eight-year-olds. Something will be going on with them, if not now, but shortly. You can just feel it.

****PIP****

I can't settle down and sleep. My mind is going around and around. This is the third night I have had no real rest. I get out of bed and head to the kitchen to make a hot chocolate, anything to try and get a sleepy vibe going.

Shoes comes pottering out of his room, fully dressed, so I know he's not resting or even trying to rest.

"You want a cup of hot chocolate?" I ask him as the kettle boils.

"Yeah, that would be nice, Pip," but he is heading for the door as he speaks.

"Where are you going?"

"I'm going to check with Chip and Mallet if all is quiet. I can ask if they want a drink too if you like?"

"Yes, that'll be good. Do you want to take Coal and let him have a quickie while you're outside?"

"No problem. Come on, Coal," he calls out.

I make us both a drink and get two cups out ready in case two more are needed. Then I hear someone shouting. I don't go out even though I am screaming to do so.

Shoes burst through the door with Coal and slams the door shut. He rushes and takes out all the lights.

"Pip, where's your Glock?" he quietly asks while low down with his weapon out.

"In my purse over by the table."

"Stay low and grab it," he states.

"What the hell is going on, Shoes?" I stay low and grab my purse, grab my Glock and kneel.

"Looks like the hitman is here Pip, he just took a shot at Mallet."

"Why try and shoot Mallet? When he is after me?" I ask him.

"If he takes us three out, then you are left with no security, leaves you wide open to be shot at," he states as he moves to peer through one of the blinds.

"Are Mallet and Chip alright?" I am starting to shake a bit now.

"Yeah, they got to cover. Mallet was near enough to get to the apartment stairs, so he legged it up. It gives him a better vantage point too."

"Shit, shit, shit, this is not good. We can't even get the police as he's crooked as shit and up in this lot," I whisper to him. "Shall I call Brand and tell him what is going on?"

"Yeah, it couldn't hurt to have extra weapons here."

The door flies open, and a man in all-black appears. Coal flies at him, but before he reaches him, the man shoots Shoes. I don't think twice and lift my weapon and fire. I hear him grunt, so I know I have hit him, and the next second, Coal is on him. Coal has him by the gun arm, thankfully, and has a damn good hold of him. He's snarling and shaking the arm for all his is worth. I grab the weapon so he cannot shoot Coal or me.

The door flies open for a second time, and I swing my Glock to the door, thank God I don't fire as its Chip. He takes in the scene quickly and tells me to call off Coal. Once we have Coal over to the other side of the trailer, Chip ties up this shooter and contacts Brand, quickly telling him what happened and to get Doc here fast.

I go to Shoes and see he was hit in his shoulder, so I grab a clean towel and put pressure on it to stop the bleeding. I hope Doc won't be too long. Thank goodness the clubhouse is just down the road.

Chip shouts to Mallet that we have the man. He comes into the trailer like a whirlwind. He's not happy and grabs the balaclava the man is wearing to see who he is and what he looks like. If he is Peter Graves, aka Ghost, we are the first people to identify him from this point.

He looks like nothing special. Just a typical day-to-day-looking man. He is even going bald, which makes me snicker. I look down at Shoes, and he also has this snide smirk on his face. Oh, we are so in tune with each other.

"I bet we were siblings in a past life, Shoes," I tell him while snickering, which sets him off too.

Chip takes a snapshot of this man and then searches his pockets. He has nothing on him apart from the weapon he used on Shoes.

The door opens, and Brand steps in with Torch behind him. Now we are getting packed in like sardines. I have to tell you. It's a bit overcrowded with alpha males, and its agitating Coal once more. He's not stopped growling since I told him to sit and stay where he is, but he is fixated on this shooter. One false move, and he will be on him again. I can see he did damage because there is blood oozing through the shirt he's wearing where Coal had hold of him.

Brand takes charge and has this ass gagged and bound even tighter, then Chip and Mallet take him off to the clubhouse, where I'm sure he will go to the basement. It must be getting a bit crowded down there. Good job, Forest was arranging for Cole Barker to be picked up.

Doc comes bowling through the door with his bag in hand.

"Is it bad? Where were you hit?" He asks Shoes while moving the towel I have been holding to the wound.

Doc fixes it up enough for Shoes to go to his medical room at the clubhouse and asks if I am hurt at all. I tell him no; I am fine and that only Shoes was hit.

Crank yanks the door open and scares the shit out of me. He comes bowling over to me and grabs me into his arms. He is rocking me as though I am a child, I am not sure if he is giving me comfort or himself, but I don't care. I put my arms around him and hang on to the hug.

Torch rubs my back as he passes and leaves the trailer. Brand tells me that Sniper is on his way, and Thunder is not far behind. They will stay with me unless I want to go to the clubhouse. I decline the offer and tell him I will be alright with my old boys and that he has work to do finding out if this man was Peter Graves and if I am now safe.

He agrees that is what he will be doing, and he'll contact Forest tomorrow to come and pick up all these bodies we seem to be collecting, thankfully, not dead bodies, I think to myself.

Once Brand and Torch leave, I settle down with Crank, and with my head resting on his shoulder, I fall asleep.

CHAPTER 19

****BRAND****

We are back at the clubhouse, and I oversee this piece of shit being placed in the basement. Chip and Mallet are staying with our 'guests' if that is what we'll call them. I tell Torch to get Pink and lock her up in her room and put a brother on her door so she cannot leave. I've not finished with her yet, and she has something to tell us, that's for sure.

Glide walks over and asks how Pip is and if this is the one called Ghost. I tell him we don't know yet, but we will know pretty quickly, even if I have to beat the holy shit out of him for the answers.

I update him on all that went down at Pip's, that Shoes was shot in the shoulder, and Coal had a good time taking a massive chunk out of the asshole's arm. At the last of the telling, he gives a good chuckle.

Taking myself down to the basement, I see Pink has been removed, and Cole Barker is looking worse for wear as he stinks with being in here so long. But I don't give a shit how much he stinks. Doc is looking at this hit man's wound, and although he is not fixing it totally, he is stabilizing it until Forest gets here and picks him up.

Chip and Mallet have decided they will do shifts on these two until they are removed as neither want any mishaps with this Ghost getting free.

Knowing everything here is under control, I go back up to my office and grab a glass of bourbon on the way. I sit behind my desk and take a few sips. Then I pick up my cell and ring Forest. I don't care what time of day it is either.

"Hello, Brand?" Forest asks when he picks up.

"Yeah, it's me, I know it's getting late, but I have news. You need to get back here tomorrow as I still have Cole Barker to pick up, but I also have your hitman. He isn't talking as we've not even bothered to ask him anything as yet. Pip shot him in the shoulder as he burst into the trailer and shot Shoes. Pip shot him on instinct, and Coal took him down and held him down, so he is a bit chewed up too," I inform him.

I feel proud of Pip and how she had handled all this. To not even pause when she had to take that shot was pretty impressive for a woman who cooks for a living.

"This happens tonight?"

"Yep, we brought him here and put him in the basement, so he's tied to a chair and going to have an uncomfortable night," I informed him. "His wound has been tended but with minimum treatment."

"No problem, Brand, as long as he is alive when I pick him up," chuckling at his own comment, "I'll organize a team now and get to you as soon as I can, sometime before lunch tomorrow, I hope."

"They'll be here. Have you got the warrants for Woolcombe, Tailor, and Keely Platt? They need to be picked up as soon as possible, I don't want them having a chance to get to Pip. You also need a warrant for Sally Tinder, who is Pink. She took money to make Pip run from the clubhouse so they could take the shot. Hence, you've got her for accessory to murder too."

"Yes, the warrant came through about an hour ago. I will get this woman added on too. All are lined up now, and we have a list of other warrants for cartel members and buyers of the women. One of my female colleagues is working on the list of women they've taken, how much they were sold for, and who to, so we can hopefully retrieve most of them that were sold. We know we won't get them all, but we'll do our best to get as many as possible," As he is sighing into the phone.

"Honestly, Brand, it's heartbreaking, but we'll get as many of these bastards as we can. We also have The Federal Ministerial Police in Mexico on board, so they have a list of the cartel they will be picking up. They won't walk away from this, and hopefully, Mexico will bring down this cartel once and for all."

"I'm going to get some rest now but will see you tomorrow when you get here," I close out the call, throw the rest of my drink down and go to my room to get some sleep.

****

The following morning, I have a shower and dressed early. I don't want to be caught on the back foot when Forest arrives. Taking myself out of my room, I see Bomber sitting outside the room at the end of the corridor.

"How long have you been on duty?" I shout to Bomber.

"Bout' five hours now, Pres."

"You want me to have a drink sent up for you? Or you got someone coming to relieve you soon?"

"Another hour, and Storm is going to come swap with me, but a drink would be nice, Pres, maybe one for Pink too as she's not had anything all night."

I give him a head nod showing him I will do that and head for the commons.

Entering the common room, I can hear what sounds like chaos going on in the kitchen. I give an eyebrow lift and look at Patch, who is sitting at one of the dining tables.

"They've been at it for an hour now, Pres," he tells me with a deadpan look on his face.

"Who has been at it?"

"Well, Dagger and June, of course," still with a deadpan expression.

"We getting any breakfast this morning then, or we gotta listen to this shit instead?"

"I had breakfast. It was alright, not as good as Pip's but far better than the bunnies used to throw at us," he states.

I wander into the kitchen, watch these two throwing insults at each other for a minute or two, then grab a plate and get myself some bacon, eggs, and toast. I don't think they even noticed I was there, which has me smirking. They will either kill each other or love each other, not sure I can wait to find out which.

As I sit down to eat, the chair next to mine is pulled back. I look to see who is sitting, and it's Ace. I lift my eyebrow at him and indicate with my fork for him to talk.

"I had a look at Pink's financials. She's had no other payment from Keely or anyone else apart from the one we know about. I knew she had a sister, so I contacted her, she told me her mother's having a lot of treatments for diabetes, and they're struggling financially. I didn't say we have Pink under house arrest, but at least we have the reason she took the money," he sighs, "I know it doesn't make it better, Pres, but at least we know she wasn't targeting Pip for any reason other than the money. She was being paid to split you two up so Woolcombe would have an easier chance of getting at Pip."

"Christ, it doesn't make it better, but I can understand why she wanted the money. But she could have come to us, and we would have helped her. All this was unnecessary. She put Pip's life on the line to help her mother keep her life."

"I will bring it up in Church Pres, and then we can decide what to do with her."

"She's going with Forest. We'll have Church once Forest has been here and picked up our 'guests."

"Oh, I forgot to tell you after everything last night, I asked Odds to see if he could find and grab Keely. We need her out the damn way as she's a risk to Pip and none of us want that. She needs to go with Forest as she'll be wanted for attempted murder," Ace informs me with an I'm sorry look on his face.

"No problem."

Before we could move from the table, we heard screaming and cursing. We both look at each other and then smirk while turning to look at the door.

The door bursts open, and Odds comes through, dragging Keely with her hands tied behind her back after him. She's cussing up a hell of a storm. He's not bothered by it at all. He doesn't even speak to us; he just walks right past and down to the basement.

I again look at Ace, he looks at me, and we both burst out laughing.

Now we hunker down and wait for Forest to arrive for all these 'guests' we have acquired.

****PIP****

Waking slowly, I have a crick in my neck for some reason. As I become aware of where I am, I have my head on Crank's lap. Oh my god, I fell asleep on Crank. I turn my head to look up and see him looking down at me with a smirk.

"Well, Pip, you sure snore," he states with a massive smile on his face.

He went from a smirk to a smile in two seconds flat, and now he is laughing out loud. How do you get out of this with any dignity, I ask myself?

I sit myself up and give Crank a timid smile, thank him for the use of his lap and kiss his cheek.

He's snickering as I walk off to freshen up and get changed. I make sure I am back in the kitchen area in a short time as I want to make sure Crank is looked after as well as he looked after me.

"I'm gonna clean up a bit now Pip, is it ok I use your bathroom?" he asks me, still smirking.

"Yes, it's through there. Clean towels are there too. You will find all the new bits in the cabinet next to the sink. Just get what you need," I tell him.

I make a fresh pot of coffee, scrambled eggs, and toast with a side of bacon and sausage. Just as I get finished, Crank comes back through. As we're eating, I ask if he has contacted anyone to see if

Shoes is alright. He informs me he had and that Shoes is fine, and Doc has him all stitched up and ready to go.

Also, he tells me Forest is coming to pick up Barker and this shooter, and then he starts laughing as he gives me the story about Odds bringing in Keely. We both have a few giggles about that.

"It must be busy in the basement Crank. Is that three or four they have in there? Maybe we need cells put in," I giggle.

"Hey, that is not a bad idea. I may put that forward in Church."

I give him the deer in the headlights look as I am not sure if he is joking or not.

"Oh, I forgot to tell you they had Pink in the basement too, but now she is under house arrest in her room," and he bursts out laughing at my shocked look.

"Do you know why she's arrested?" I say with a slight giggle.

"Well, Torch wasn't happy at all about what went down. He knew something was going on, so he pressed Ace to find out, which of course he did, and it turns out Pink took the money as her mother has a diabetes issue, she needed money for treatment. But if she had asked, we would have helped her Pip, so it boils down to her throwing you under the bus to save her mother."

"Flipping heck Crank, I would have helped her too if she had asked. Now I would not piss on her if she was on fire," and I look up at Crank with this disgusting face on, he just bursts out laughing again.

"Damn Pip, I love spending time with you, always a smile or a laugh to be had when you're around."

Crank's cell rings, and he picks it up from where he had it sitting on the table. Looking at me, he tells me to get a move on we're going to the clubhouse. Forest has turned up with a team to pick up our guests.

I quickly put Coal out for a quick run and then shut him in the trailer. I shout to Cali, who is just going up the stairs to the apartment, that we are going to the clubhouse, and Coal is in the trailer. He gives us the thumbs up, so we make our way to my SUV.

We pull up at the clubhouse, and Crank and I wander in. We are a bit late, by the looks of it, or they just didn't bother waiting for us to start any meeting.

Sandy shouts to me, and I look over at her.

"They only went into Church two minutes ago, Pip. They said for you both to go straight in when you arrive."

"Thanks, Sandy."

Crank doesn't wait for an invite. He just opens the door and barrels into Church holding my elbow to make sure I don't linger behind.

I see Forest and a few FBI suits I don't know, including a woman. He welcomes us to the meeting and lists the warrants he has to hand in and one for Sally Tinder. I have to ask as I have no idea who that is. When I am told Pink, I raise my eyebrows as to who would have guessed she was a 'Sally.'

"What are you arresting her for, Bill?" I ask as I'm not sure what the heck is going on with this one.

"She is under arrest for accessory to commit murder. She knew what they were going to do, Pip. She took the money and set Brand up so you would run, giving them the chance to pick you off once you were clear of the clubhouse."

"Do you have everyone arrested, or have you still to pick some up?" I ask, hoping he says he has them all.

"We don't have Woolcombe as yet. Bruce Tailor, I got a message they picked him up earlier this morning. Keely Platt is here for pick up, along with Cole Barker and the unknown hitman, who I will chat with in a minute or two. The rest on our list will be picked up by various agents across the US and officials in Mexico."

I wish this were all over, I'm thinking to myself, but fingers crossed it is coming to an end soon.

"Do you need me to stay any longer? If not, I would like to get back to my trailer as I have quite a few things to do in the next couple of days."

Brand steps towards me, and Forest nods. Brand places his hand on my back and guides me out of Church, but he calls Odds to follow us. It's alright with him if I leave.

"I want you to go with Pip back to the trailer. Make sure she's alright, and when Church is finished and Shades gets back to work, you can leave."

"You alright with that, Pip?" he asks, which is a first as he usually just tells me what is happening.

"Yep, no problem," and with that, we go to my SUV, and I hand over my keys to Odds, who's holding his hand out, 'Men.' As we pull out of the clubhouse drive, I give a slight wave to Brand who is watching us leave.

Brand re-enters the clubhouse to finalize Bill Forest's visit.

CHAPTER 20

####*PIP*###

Three days after everyone was picked up by Bill Forest, the place has become quiet, which is lovely. We are still waiting for Woolcombe to be found. He seems to have gone underground.

I have advertisements out for staff for the restaurant, and the work on the apartment is moving along nicely. They are plastering it all now as the wiring was completed a couple of days ago.

The mail carrier delivered the parcel I was waiting for, and a large envelope from Larry Thomas with my will amended for a second time, plus another legal document I wanted.

I still have the list I need to discuss with Brand about getting help for the clubhouse as poor Sandy is run ragged with only her left. Molly is helping as much as possible, too, but it is not easy on either of them, and I know Trigger is getting fed up with Molly working too many hours.

Knowing all this, I grab my cell and ring Brand.

"Hi Pip, everything alright?" he asks when he answers after four rings.

"Yes, everything's fine. I need to come over to the clubhouse as I have a list to discuss with you if you can find the time. If it's possible at all, I have an announcement to make to a couple of people in the club, and I thought it would be nice if everyone were there when I did that. Would it be possible to do that, do you think?" I ask while biting my lip as I am nervous about it in case it's not appreciated anyway.

"I have no problem with that, Pip. You are loved here, and everyone would be happy to hear any announcement you would have. What time should I ask people to be here?"

"What about seven? Would that be alright? I need Sandy and Shoes to be there please if you could make that happen, oh and Shades," I ask.

"Yes, I can do that, Pip," he responds, sounding intrigued, but I'm not telling him more as I want this to be a surprise for everyone.

"Thanks' Brand. I really appreciate it. I will be over in half an hour with this list if that is convenient?"

"I'll be here, Pip."

I cut off the call and take Coal for a quickie, grab a minute to freshen up, and pack my Glock, notepad, and cell in my purse, ready to leave. I should make it on time if I don't linger.

I walk into the clubhouse, and the Old Boys shout me over. I head over to them and give them all a kiss on the cheek and a cheesecake I made yesterday, especially to spoil them when I came today.

"That is just for you four," I tell them with a big smile on my face.

"You are a star, and we love you, babe," Thunder says as he headed for the kitchen. To grab plates and cutlery, I'm sure.

I hear my name called and turn to see Brand standing at the entrance to the corridor, so I walk over and follow him into the office.

"So, what have you got for me, Pip?"

"Well, after speaking to Molly and some brothers, also that Sandy will be leaving at some stage to work for me, we felt it was needed to get some staff here to do some cleaning, cooking, and serving behind the bar." I get my notepad out to remind me to cover everything.

"One thing Molly said which I thought warranted your thought was that instead of having bunnies to serve behind the bar, why don't you have the prospects do shifts there as well as gate duty, etc.? It would help the brothers get to know them better and more quickly. It would also let the prospects see what club life is about."

"You need at least two for the kitchen and three for general cleaning, so a five minimum would be needed to help the clubhouse run smoothly. So many chores to do within the clubhouse with so many brothers living here that even another two helpers would not hurt."

"I agree, Pip, and I'm bringing it to Church that we don't have bunnies here anymore, we have fortnightly parties in-club instead, then if anyone wants to mingle sexually, they can, but it will be like just going to a club anywhere."

He looks to see if I have an opinion, which I don't on this issue.

"After what happened to Shades and then with Pink, I honestly think it's time to stop having easy pussy in the club. It will get voted on, so it will be a majority decision."

"That is a good way to do it, Brand. Then everyone can say what they think too," I shuffle my feet a bit and gather my bits and pieces. "Right, I'm going to dash, and I will see you about seven this evening. Thanks for listening, Brand, and I'm sure the security team will vet people for the places well."

"Thanks, Pip, for getting opinions and bringing all this to me. It's easier when I'm brought the facts so I can put it forward without having to research it all myself."

We go through the commons, and I wave to everyone as I go past, shouting, see you later to them all.

Brand tells me to take care as Woolcombe is still at large, and he will see me later.

Arriving back at the trailer, I see Shoes sitting on the trailer steps while Coal's running around enjoying himself.

"Can I speak to you, Shoes, when you're finished with Coal?" I ask him as I squeeze past into the trailer.

"Yeah, two minutes is all, Pip, and I'll be with you."

Grabbing a tin of juice and the parcel that arrived earlier, I get comfy at the dining table, and I only wait a short while before Shoes comes in.

"Can you sit while I talk to you a minute, please?" I state, trying my no-nonsense voice.

"Yeah, no problem, Pip," looking a bit nervous.

"You remember when we had that discussion about you trading with more than just a few dollars, and you said you would think about it, well I thought about it, and I like the idea more and more so I have a gift for you," at this point, I push the parcel towards him.

He looks apprehensive now, and I start nibbling my lip, getting stressed myself.

"Oh my god, Pip, a brand-new top model laptop," he beams

He has a pink glow all over his face, so he is embarrassed or just really happy.

"Well, I decided that to do the job well, you need a top-of-the-line laptop so you can do what it is you do without worry and plenty of whatever you need to save your information," I state, not knowing what the heck I am talking about, I'm just trying to repeat what the salesman said.

"Pip, you don't know what you're talking about, do you?" he says, laughing.

"No damn clue," I replied, laughing.

"Thank you so much Pip, I will do my best, and I will keep a record so I can show you what I'm doing."

At this point, I put my hand up to stop him.

"No, I don't want any proof, I trust you implicitly, and you just do whatever you do, we go 50/50, I'll give you my bank details, and I will get a nice surprise when I get my statements," I grab my purse looking for the envelope in there.

"This is for you also to get you started. I had to ask Ace your real name" I giggle at that.

He takes and opens the envelope and sees a check for $100,000 made out in his name. He looks at me in utter disbelief, but I just give him what I hope is my sweetest smile.

"Thank you, Pip, for trusting me and being my dear friend," hugging me as he says this.

I hug him back, thinking you're going to be more than my dear friend.

"Okay, you got things to do with that laptop, and I've got some bits to do before I make us a meal. We are at the clubhouse tonight at seven. Will you be able to drive me over, or are you going to be out?" hoping he can drive me over. I'm still nervous on my own.

"I can drive you over, Pip, as it's my day off today."

"Did you speak to you know who? Did you get that paperwork signed? Did she accept the $30,000 I gave you?" I ask, with all my fingers crossed.

"Oh yes, I forgot, I have to go over there at six to do the pickup or get someone else to do it." he smiles broadly at me.

With that, I go into my bedroom and sit on the bed, rubbing my hands, thinking and hoping all will come together well tonight.

After a while, I stroll out and see Shoes engrossed in the laptop, so I quietly take myself out of the trailer, so I don't disturb him.

I go up to the apartment and see everyone has made excellent progress. They are all working so hard to get things done for me.

I ask if they all want a cold one as I had the first delivery to the restaurant, which just happened to be wines, beers, and spirits, so I had plenty of cold bottles.

They all said yes, they would love just the one, and I pop back down and grab us all one. I run back up and hand one out to each of them and tell them how much I appreciate all the hard work. I also ask if they will be at the clubhouse tonight. Thankfully they all say yes, including Shades, which makes me inwardly grin.

We finish our drinks, and I take all the empties downstairs and head back to the trailer.

I toss together a stir-fry; we enjoy that with an iced tea and chat.

After we feed Coal and give him a run, I excuse myself to refresh and change. I wear my skinny jeans, biker boots and my soft pink sweater.

"You ready yet, Shoes?" I ask when I go into the kitchen area.

"Yeah, I just need to check who is on patrol. Are we taking Coal with us?"

"Oh, yes, let's take him, he loves the old boys, and he hasn't been out for ages," I quickly agree.

While Shoes is outside checking patrol, I grab the legal papers and put them in my purse, I make sure I pick up the vehicle keys, and then I think to double-check where my Glock is as I want it in my purse for the moment.

"Ready, Pip? I have Coal in the SUV."

"I'm ready too, so let's go."

When we get to the clubhouse, everyone seems to be around. It looks like Brand did an excellent job at getting them all here for my announcement. Now I see them all. I'm damn nervous as this could go pear-shaped.

I roam for a minute, saying hello to people, then see Brand at the bar. Making my way to him, I take a deep breath and ask him if he will get everyone's attention for me.

"SHUT IT," he bellows at everyone, to which the place goes silent.

"Pip has something to say," he proclaims.

I make sure I'm standing in the central bar area to place my papers on the bar.

"Thank you, everyone, for coming tonight. I asked Brand if he would get you all here so I could say a few things. I hope what I'm about to do is received in a good way as I don't mean anything untoward by what I'm about to do." I'm shaking with nerves now.

"Firstly, will Sandy come to stand with me, please?"

When she's standing with me looking worried, I take her hand and smile.

"Sandy, in the kitchen one day, we were talking about improving our lives and what we would have liked to have done, and you told me you wanted to be an accountant but never had the money to go to college and do that," I shuffle a bit "Well you are going to college now, you can do it online, or you can physically go to college," I pass her a folder with both those options for her to choose from. "All you have to do is choose. Once you're an accountant, I was hoping you could work for me and do the books at the restaurant. I'm sure Brand will drag you in to do business books too," said while laughing.

Sandy is crying, she looks up at me and throws her arms around me, thanking me, and we will talk about it later.

"Next, can Shades come to stand with me, please?"

Shades strides over to me with a mystified look on his face, but at that moment, Tyler and Odds come bursting through the door. Odds shouts, sorry we're late.

Shades picks Tyler up, but I ask him to hand him to Odds for a moment. Which he does while giving me a wicked look.

"I have a folder for you also, Shades, and I hope it holds the world of happiness for you," and I hand him the folder.

Shades takes and opens the folder. He reads the papers inside and then lunges to pick me up and hug me so fiercely I can hardly breathe. He's crying into my shoulder, and I just hold him to me until he gets himself under control.

"Thank you so much, Pip. This means everything to me. You have no idea what you've done."

"Yeah, I think I do, and I was happy to do it. Now you best tell everyone else what you have."

Shades turns to everyone in the clubhouse and yells out, "My son is mine, only mine, he's signed over, all parental rights from Babs is now nil and void."

The whole building bursts into whistles, foot stomps, and congratulations.

"Lastly, can Shoes step up, please?" I call out.

Shoes steps forward, looking majorly awkward, but I take his hand and pick up the last folder on the bar.

"This folder is special to me as well. I hope as it will be to Chris, which is his real name everyone," laughter follows this comment "I just want to say welcome Brother," and I hand him the folder.

Shoes takes the folder while giving me an odd look. He reads the legal document with a large X showing where to sign. He looks at me, and a tear runs down his cheek. I wipe it with my thumb while a tear runs down my cheek, and he wipes that with his thumb.

"Are you going to be my brother? Are you going to be Christopher East instead of Christopher Thomas?" and I hold my breath.

"Too fucking right, I will," and he picks me up and spins me for all he is worth.

The clubhouse is alive with congratulations, back slaps, and hugs. It's a glorious thing to see.

Crank walks up to me, wraps his arms around me, and whispers, "You are the most beautiful human being I have ever met, and I'm proud to call you my friend."

"You're more than a friend to me, Crank. You're my family," I hug him tightly while a tear runs down my cheek. I lost my parents but have found a new family here.

Crank looks down at me and then around the clubhouse and shouts, "Let's Party!" and that is precisely what we do.

CHAPTER 21

****PIP****

It's been a week since we had the party after all my announcements. Shades has Tyler living at the clubhouse now, and the old boys are watching over him whenever needed. I caught Shades whistling this morning, to which he gave me a crooked grin when I pointed and laughed at him.

Sandy will do the online accounting course as she wants to stay and help at the clubhouse until they have new people doing the cooking and cleaning. She will have to go into the next town to do her final exams as it has to be in a classroom environment, but that is not a problem.

Shoes and I are building our sibling relationship, which is just great as I am playing sister tricks on him, and as yet, he's a bit shy to return them, so I'm making the most of it while I can. I just turned all his white briefs pink, on purpose, of course, much to his frustration when he sees them in his wash pile. I was good and had purchased him all new white ones ready.

He also is doing great with his trading, and we both have doubled my original outlay amount. How he has done that so quickly is beyond me, but I don't care. He is happy and enjoying life, for the first time, I think.

Speaking of the devil, here he is back from his latest prospect duty.

"Do you want an iced tea?" I ask as he enters the trailer.

"No thanks, Pip, I'm going out again in a little while."

"I've been thinking about you buying a house, and I don't want you to move away from me when we just have each other. So, after thinking about it, when the new apartment is built, why don't you live there?" I hold my breath as I want him near. "Or, you could build a house on the back property near where I'll be building mine?"

"That actually would work out great, Pip," he hums a bit, thinking, "Yeah, I'll have the apartment, and then whenever I want, I can build."

He comes over and gives me a hug and a kiss on my head.

"Alright, I am off again but will be back to eat with you."

I let Coal out so he can have a run-around, grab myself an iced tea and sit on the trailer step enjoying the crispness of the day. It's getting colder now, and Thanksgiving is nearly here.

Tomorrow I will be doing all the interviews for the restaurant, and I offered to do for the clubhouse too. Brand will be here to do them with me as I didn't want to employ people he may not like or know something that would eliminate them.

I heard from Liza this morning, and she's starting to wind down her catering over in Nebraska, so by the time the apartment is finished, she should be ready to move in. Things are moving along nicely, and I'm excited to open the restaurant.

My cell starts to ring, so I grab it after I see it is Larry contacting.

"Hello Larry"

"Good afternoon, Pip, I'm ringing to let you know your amended *'will'* will be with you tomorrow. I did it by special delivery."

"Great, thank you. You have been great through all this Larry, and I appreciate it."

"Anytime, Pip, your parents were great friends of mine, and I would do anything for them as they would have for me."

"I know the practice is closed, and I don't want to be involved with it anymore, so can you see about putting it on the market for sale?"

"I will speak to Bill for you and see if we can do that, it should be okay as you have no involvement in any of the Woolcombe trouble, but we'll make sure. Also, there is all that money in those accounts that will need going through because some of that is legitimate practice dollars he stole."

"Will you deal with that, Larry, or do I need someone else?"

"No, I can deal with it as I have an accountant who can work with the FBI to clear all this mess up."

"Great, keep me informed, please. Take care, Larry," and I close the call.

I run over to the apartment to see how near they are to finalizing as the furniture is now all paid for, and they just need me to give them a date to deliver. It will be stunning, I am sure. I have chosen all ivory and terracotta colors.

"Helloooo!" I shout as I reach the top of the stairs and open the door.

Oh, my, the kitchen looks fantastic, they just have a few pieces to finish, but it's stunning.

"Hi Pip, you want to check out the bedroom we just got finished," Shades asks.

We go through the lounge area into the bedroom, and I just love it. They have fitted everything in, and there is plenty of space left over for the bed. I ordered a queen size. I'm sure it will fit and leave enough room to wander around it. All it needs is the shades and light fixtures and will be completed.

"Amazing Shades, you have done such a magnificent job all around. You have all worked so hard and achieved exactly what I wanted. Thank you." I hug him and then dash for the bathroom.

"Yay, it looks gorgeous. The whole room looks warm and welcoming, and the bath and separate shower fit in perfectly on that wall," I say without even checking if he has followed me through.

"Yes, we are so happy with how it all has turned out, Pip. I got three workers in from a friend's company in the next town to give us a boost this last week, and they worked out well, so I'll use them again."

He updates me on the finishing touches they have to do, and I give him the details so he can arrange for the rest of the furniture to be delivered. He also gives me the floor plan for the extension, the catering business, and the office with the second apartment above. I glance over it and give him the go-ahead whenever he's ready.

"I think you should move into the apartment until your house is built Pip, it will be safer than the trailer, especially with winter coming," he says.

"No, I want Shoes in this apartment, and if it gets bad, I will ask Brand if I can have a room at the clubhouse. I do want Shoes settled with his own place. He's suffered so much that I want him to have some luxury in his life now. I want him to know he's cared for and important."

"I think he knows that Pip, he's your Bro' now after all," he said with a grin on his face.

We wrap it up for now, and I head back to the trailer.

"Pip, you busy?"

I turn to see who called me and see Brand sitting astride his bike at the side of the restaurant.

"Hi Brand," I shout as I walk over to see what he's doing.

"I had a call from Bill Forest and told him I would update you on what's going on."

"Oh," I am a bit surprised he hadn't called me himself, but it doesn't matter who informs me. "Come on in the trailer and have a drink while you update me," I say as I start to head toward the trailer.

Once I have placed an iced tea for each of us on the table and sat, I'm ready to hear any news he can throw at me, but studying him, he doesn't look upset, so I hope everything has gone as Forest wanted.

"Woolcombe is still in the wind. Unfortunately, they have had a couple of sightings around Nebraska, so he's sticking around home for the moment, but they just keep missing him. The hitman is known as Ghost, but he was also an ex-FBI agent; it turns out, he was recognized when they took him in by his old partner. He's going on trial for multiple murders," Brand takes a deep breath and continues, "Keely and Pink are charged with accessory to murder and Cole Barker for attempted murder. The Mexican law enforcement has arrested twenty-two cartel members for murder, trafficking, and drug charges. The Mexican government is delighted with how many they have taken down for this and are still looking for women that may not have been rescued yet."

"Oh, my god," I blow out a breath because I'm still thinking about what he has told me, and it's mind-blowing.

"The financials that Woolcombe has are under investigation, but it looks like the offshore account is the one where he kept the trafficking dollars. Forest said that if that is right, then as Woolcombe is going to prison for life, once they catch him, the rest will go to you as he has no family" he looks at me with raised eyebrows.

I don't know what to say, so I just keep staring at him.

"Do you have any idea how much they're talking about, Pip? The practice he ripped off was millions, and the drug money is gone, it was paid to the cartel apart from what he made himself, and they can't say how much that was because those records were not intact, what is left is what the FBI will pay to you once everything is completed. Forest estimates $18 million." he looks at me, waiting for a reaction.

I don't do or say anything. I just sit staring at him as I had no idea and have enough money to last forever anyway.

"You alright, Pip?" he asks and takes hold of my hand.

"Yeah, I'm just trying to understand all you've said," I take some deep breaths to calm my racing heart. "Do they know who killed my parents?"

"Yes, the Ghost said Woolcombe did that himself. He bragged to him about it," he held my other hand now too. "I'm sorry, Pip."

I nod to him and just let the tears flow.

After all this, the day passed pretty smoothly. Shoes came back in time so that we could eat together. I filled him in on what I had learned, he hugged me and told me everything would be alright.

He even called me Sis' for the first time, which made me cry much to his distress until I burst out laughing at the look on his face.

****BRAND****

The interviews went pretty well. We have picked up four women to clean and cook at the clubhouse and a man who is retired at 45 due to an injury in his leg. Still, he's an experienced barman, even had an establishment at one time, so he'll be able to do inventory and orders for supplies, taking some work off my shoulders.

One of the women is 43 years of age, and she's run her own bed and breakfast business, so I put her in charge of the others, a sure way of me not having to talk about toilets, showers, and cooking.

Pip picked up two cooks for the daytime meals and a woman who has only three months left to attain her chef certification. She also picked up four waitresses and two waiters.

She was buzzing when we were finished and opened some bubbly, which she took round for everyone on the property to celebrate. She loves to spoil people and interact. It's endearing.

When she gets back with the empty bottles of bubbly, I grab her arm and tell her to change into her jeans and a jacket as she is coming for a ride with me on the bike. She looks surprised but bolts off to get ready, so she must want to get on the bike.

I make sure her helmet fits snugly and then straddle the bike. I tell her how to get on and put her feet on the pegs. I grab her hands and wrap them around my waist and ask her to hang on tight, to lean when I lean and just enjoy.

We head out into the country where I know she'll enjoy the scenery, and I know an ice cream place a couple of towns over where we can sit outside on a bench, so I head that way. About ten minutes into the ride, I feel her relax and start to enjoy herself. She throws her arms in the air and laughs loudly, making me laugh with her. I kick up our speed a little, which has her grabbing hold once more.

At the ice cream place, we grab our order and sit on one of the benches. It is a pleasant day, a bit cooler as it is Autumn now. We chat about the restaurant opening, and I agree with her that Thanksgiving would be a tremendous opening date. She, however, doesn't want to be available for the public on Thanksgiving. She wants all the club to come for dinner. I ask if she is sure, and she is adamant, whatever she wants, I am happy to oblige, and I am sure everyone will be glad to come to eat.

Once we get back to the bike, I turn into her and hold her face in my hands. Bending down to her face, I give her time to move or say something, but she looks at me with want in her eyes, so I continue down and place my lips over hers. Once she moans, I cannot help myself, and I just kiss the shit outta her. When I next look at her, she has a glazed look and beautiful pink cheeks.

"Do you want me, Pip? Do you want us to be an 'us'? I could happily love you for the rest of my life," I just lay my cards on the table and hope she can see that.

"Yes, I want there to be an 'us' Brand, but you have to want me and just me as I won't stand for any cheating. I'm not made that way. We either go all in, or we don't go in at all," she tells me, but they are the sweetest words she could have ever said.

"Come on, let's get back. I want you in my room, naked, hot, and wanting," I tell her, and I enjoy the blush that flowed up her face from her neck.

CHAPTER 22

****BRAND****

Once we arrive back at the clubhouse, I take Pip's hand and lead her to my room. As soon as the door closes, I step into her. She takes steps back until she has the door at her back. I place my hands on both sides of her face and lower my lips to hers.

This is not a hurried kiss. I am making love to her mouth. My tongue dances with hers; she moans into my mouth, which tickles my tongue. She tastes sweet and spicy. I will never get enough. I moan into her mouth in response.

I slide my hand up and down her side, lifting her shirt until I can feel her skin, hot and smooth under my hand. I cup her breast and run my thumb over her tightened nipple through her bra. This is not enough. I release her and help rid her of her clothes, then remove my own. We are now both taking our fill of each other's naked bodies.

I lay her down on the bed and climb on next to her, looking my fill as I do so. She reaches out and digs her fingers into my hair, dragging me down to kiss me. My hands run down her body, feeling the silkiness of her skin, and I hook her leg over my hip, running my hand up and over her butt cheek.

Kissing along her neck and down to take a nipple into my mouth and suck and roll my tongue, taking my fill, she arches her back and throws her head back, moaning with pleasure as she does so.

Running my hand down, I finally touch the folds of her sex, gently rubbing her clit, making her jump and moan. Her thighs start to tremble, and her moans increase which sounds beautiful to my ears.

I cannot wait any longer and line myself up. I'm hot and hard and push steadily into her wetness. I keep pressing into her heat until I am fully seated. I pause to give her time to be comfortable with my size, and then I start to move.

Placing my forearms at the sides of her and kissing her hungrily as my strokes increase. She lifts her legs and wraps them around my hips, letting me go even further into her.

The muscles in my legs are starting to tremble, I can feel the tingling start running up my spine, and I cannot hold off much longer. I glide my hand down her front and reach for her clit, gently rubbing until it takes her over, and at the same time, I let myself go, we climax together.

I don't move. I just hold myself over her and kiss her telling her how much I love touching her and tasting her lips. I run my fingers through her hair. She's stroking my back and sides.

I feel myself hardening once more, and by the look of surprise then a soft smile, she has no problem with that either. I start to move slowly and kiss her neck, shoulders, and breasts. My hands are roaming over her body, and I enjoy the feel of her skin.

She tries to push me faster and bites my shoulder. My response to that is to pull out of her and flip her over quickly, then push back in again, hard. I pull her up onto her hands and knees.

I lick up her spine and run my hand up her side, rubbing over her butt and down her thigh. I push between her shoulders, so she is down at the front and ass up in the air with me starting to pound into her.

We lose ourselves to the pleasure of the moment, the moans, sweetly saying each other's name, then she screams my name before she starts to collapse to the bed. I hold her in place for a few more strokes before I moan her name at completion.

Once our breathing evens out, I pull out of her and wrap my arms around her.

"You alright Pip."

"Yeah, I'm great, that was great," she giggles, "When can we do it again?"

"We can do that again very soon, and often for the rest of our lives." and I mean it with every breath of my body. She's mine, and she won't be going anywhere. I cannot live without her now.

"I love you, Pip," I exclaim quietly, kissing her forehead.

"I love you too," she responds, snuggling into my chest.

"You're my old lady now, Pip, no going back, you're with me until we die, no divorce, no running off, we work through any problems we have together. I'll order your property kutte, and you wear it whenever you're out and about, and if we have other clubs here at the clubhouse, it will keep you safe at all times."

"Yeah, that sounds good."

"I want eight kids too," I say this to see what response I get.

"Eight kids, I don't think so, I don't mind three or even four, but not eight." she quickly tells me with a huff at even the thought of eight. She's giggling as she knows I'm playing with her to get a reaction.

This moment in my life changes everything. I have my old lady, I am President of my club, and I hope in the not too far off distance we'll start a family.

I pray nothing will spoil what we have now.

****PIP****

The following two weeks pass by well. I'm spending most nights with Brand at the clubhouse. I don't think having sex in the trailer with Shoes in the next room is a good sister move. He's happy about Brand and I getting together, but I had to smile when he stands chest to chest, looking up at Brand and telling him he is a dead man if he hurts me. Brand responded he would give him the weapon to get the job done if he did.

We have the apartment finished, so whenever Liza is ready, she can move in. I have not heard from her, so I will send her a text to let her know. The apartment is stunning, with beautiful wood floors that shine in the light, small chandelier light fittings, and the queen size bed fit perfectly. The ivory leather suite in the lounge looks stunning with all the terracotta-colored throw cushions, and the kitchen is modern, clean-looking, with all the appliances needed.

The enclosed stairway won't be built until they have finished the extension as it will be a joint staircase between the two apartments. They will both have high-security main doors for the apartments so no one can enter without being permitted. The stairs also will have a security camera at the bottom door and above each apartment door. Why take risks these days is my motto.

My cell buzzed, letting me know I received a text message and it is an unknown number. I hesitate to read it or not, but I am nosy, so I did, then I scream.

Obituary – Piper East
This will be you in a short space of time bitch

I drop my cell and step away from it as though it will burst into flames. Cali bursts into the trailer with his weapon drawn. He checks all around then waits for me to tell him what's wrong. Cali never pushes, he is such a happy person, but he is highly intelligent and knows when to wait.

He notices my cell on the floor, so he picks it up and sees the message. Looking me over, he asks if I'm alright, and I tell him I'm okay but was shocked.

Cali rings Spider and tells him what happened and forwards the message to him, but Spider wants my cell to see if he can find out where it came from. We are not stupid; we know it's going to be Woolcombe. He eventually will come out of hiding.

Putting on the coffee machine gives me something to do while we wait for Spider to arrive. I get cups ready and grab the donuts I had Shoes bring when he was in town this morning.

I hear the bikes and know it's more than Spider, so look out the trailer door and see Brand and Ace too. I grab extra cups and start pouring.

Coal is excited to see everyone, but he is not jumping around. He is just wagging the tip of his tail. He is so tuned to my emotions that he seems to read situations as they are warranted.

Brand comes through the door and wraps me in his arms, breathing me in, and I do the same in return. He gives me so much comfort with just his smell of leather and musk aftershave. I would know it was him by his smell blindfolded.

We all take a seat apart from Spider, who's looking at my phone and plugging it into his laptop. He has so many programs he runs at the office that I am surprised he has not just taken off with my cell, but I suppose he may do that yet.

"Pip, the text came from the tower in Nebraska, so we can presume it is Woolcombe, but he is not here. He is not any nearer than he was the last few weeks. Can you try not to panic, as that is exactly what he wants you to do? He's trying to play with your head." Spider states.

He is still looking at the cell and checking with the laptop as he speaks to me, he is such a serious man, and I hope one day he finds someone who will lighten him up and give him the joy in his life he so deserves, he looks after everyone, he takes our security to heart, and it drains him at times.

"I think you need to stay at the clubhouse full time, for now, Pip, or even move into the apartment until your friend turns up," Ace says. "It's not as secure in the trailer as you having solid bricks around you."

I can agree to that, and although I am happy to stay at the clubhouse now, I will be making Thanksgiving dinner for everyone in a week, and I have a lot of deliveries coming that I will need to sign off on and then unpack.

"Right, I am going to stay at the apartment because I have a hectic week, and I don't have the time to be driving back and forth to the clubhouse," I state, rubbing my hands together as my nerves have still not settled down, "If you are all okay with that then that is what I will do. Will you stay with me, Brand?"

"Wouldn't be anywhere else," he responds.

****LIZA****

I am starting to pack my apartment up and have handed in my notice on my lease for the end of the month. My contract with the catering company is up at the same time, so I can just get in my car and drive as soon as I can. I cannot wait. I am so looking forward to being with my BFF, Pip. It has been far too long since we were living in each other's lives; keeping in touch by our cell phones is just not enough.

My cell rings, and I jump, not wanting to see who it is, but I have to as I have work today, so it could be related to my job. I see it is Bennett, my boss, my creepy as shit boss, who won't take no for an answer.

"Hello!" I have found it wise to say as little as possible where this ass is concerned.

"I need you into work an hour early Liza, one of the girls has called in sick." he spits at me.

It seems he is having a bad day, but I don't care anymore; the job is just not worth it. If I could leave today to get to Pip, I would, but this piece of garbage would call me out on breach of contract, which would cost me dearly.

"I will be at the office on time. Will I be catering or in the kitchen?" I have to know about the outfit I will wear.

"Kitchen." and he cuts off the call.

'*Asshole, shithead, prick,*' I mutter to myself as I go into the bathroom to have a quick shower before getting ready for work.

Arriving at work, I place my purse and coat in my locker and head for the kitchen. When I get there, I'm surprised as no one is here. There is no sign of any catering being prepared. I head to the office and knock on the door.

"Come in," Bennett calls out.

"I think there is a mistake as there is no one in the kitchen, and by the looks, no catering happening today?" I question as I move into the room.

Bennett comes around his desk, placing papers on it as he does so. I patiently wait for him to say whatever bullshit he is going to spout.

"I'm asking if you're going to back down now, Liza, and come to me as I told you to?" he snappily asks.

"No, I am not. I have told you and told you I am not having an affair with you. You have a wife and children. I am not a mistress and never will be." I calmly state, my heart is beating wildly, as I am damn worried now as to what the hell is going on.

"Okay, Liza, your loss," he states as he lifts his hand and brings it back to punch me in the face.

Before I can get out of his way, he has landed another three, and I cannot see for the tears in my eyes, and the pain in my face is horrendous. I lift my arms to cover my head, allowing him to punch me in the ribs, which takes my breath and takes me to the floor. He commences to kick me. He gets one to the back of my head where I see stars, and then everything goes black.

The next time I open my eyes, I am in the hospital and have been here for over a week. Apparently, my brain swelled slightly with the injury to the back of my head, and the surgeon kept me under to give my brain a chance to calm as he didn't want to operate unless he had to.

"Now you're awake can you tell us your name?" the surgeon asks.

I blink at him, screw up my face, and think, but I have no idea who the hell I am. Panic starts to rise in my chest and tears come from nowhere, and I scream. I feel a sharp prick and then nothing, once again darkness.

CHAPTER 23

****PIP***

The week is busy. I'm ensuring I have everything for the Thanksgiving meal and the orders for the week commencing when the restaurant opens to the public.

Jenna has done a fabulous job, and she is a bit of an organizing freak, so I will talk to her about working for me in the office. I could use her skills, although her artwork would have to take a step back, which I am not sure she will want to do. It's worth asking, and I can compromise with her doing fewer hours if needed.

I am worried that I am getting no replies from Liza. She is supposed to be here for Thanksgiving and then helping me in the restaurant. This is not like her, and I don't have a number for her boss, only the business. I am getting a *call back at a less busy time* message each time I ring.

If I don't get a reply in a few more days, I'll speak to Brand about going over to find her. I worry that Nebraska will take me near Woolcombe. I will risk it for Liza as I have this horrid feeling something is wrong.

Leaving the apartment, I go down the stairs and see something on the bottom step. What is a box doing there, I am thinking? I reach it and notice it has my name on it. How odd, nobody has mentioned any delivery, and it is not even my full name and address, just my first name.

Picking it up, I walk into the kitchen and place it on the counter nearest the door. I rip it open, wondering if it is something I ordered and have forgotten about. My mind is blank as to what it could be.

I look in and scream, it is a chicken, and it has had its head chopped off. Oh my God, there is an envelope on the side of the box.

Cali and Shades rush into the kitchen, hearing me scream. They are both holding a weapon and looking around for the threat. I just stand pointing at the box, and I cannot even say anything. The shock is making me shake.

Cali looks in the box and starts muttering curses. He grabs the envelope and rips it open.

Pip,

You have it coming. I will chop your head off just like that chicken, you have cost me far too much, and now I am your judge, jury, and executioner.

You won't see me coming, but I am here.

S.W.

Shades rips the note from Cali's hand then grabs his cell, leaving the kitchen at the same time.

I look at Cali. He just walks up to me, puts his arms around me, and holds me for what feels like forever.

"It'll be alright, Pip. We will keep you safe," he continues to hold me even when Shades re-enters the kitchen. "You have to consider canceling the Thanksgiving dinner, Pip, until we get this bastard strung up."

I am taken from Cali's arms and wrapped up in Shades. He is talking to me, but I do not hear it. Everything is white noise at the moment.

"Pip, you listening?" Shades asks me.

"I'm sorry, Shades, I didn't hear what you said."

"It's alright, Brand is on his way and half the brothers," he says this chuckling, "You have the brothers wanting to protect you Pip, did you have some magic dust you sprinkled on them all." He asks, laughing.

We hear bikes, so we know the cavalry has arrived.

Brand enters the kitchen and makes a beeline for me, taking me from Shades, wrapping me uptight in his arms, and kissing my head.

"You okay, Pip?" he asks while breathing me in, "I'm gonna kill him when I find him."

"No, you aren't; we need him to go down for this, so he suffers for a long time," I say.

I don't know how the hell I'm going to stay safe until we catch him.

Spider and Ace walk in with a laptop each, and they use one of the counters to set up and start clicking on their keyboards.

"Got him," Ace says. "It's a kid, can't be much older than fourteen."

We all look at the image he has on his laptop, taken from the security cam on the back wall of the building. It seems the amount of cameras Spider used was warranted after all.

"We need to set a damn trap for him, catch him off guard, make sure we grab him before he gets to me," I state while removing myself from Brand and walking back and forth, pinching my thumb and finger on the top of my nose.

"No, definitely not," Brand snaps, "Not happening, Pip."

"Yes, happening, I need to get my life back, and I won't have it until he is taken down one way or another."

I respond, still pacing back and forth, trying to think how the hell we can trap him.

"I think it is a good idea," Spider chimes in, "If we set the trap, at least we will be in control. As it is, we are on the back foot all the damn time. We need to be the ones calling the shots from now on."

"I don't like it, and anything could go wrong." Brand states and he is worried about this idea.

"Why don't we speak to Bill Forest? He wants him caught as much as we do."

"I agree, we need to do that, Pip, and he may have an idea to catch this bastard." Ace states while packing up his laptop.

We decide that is the next step, see what Forest can come up with.

****BRAND****

I leave Pip at the apartment with Shades and Cali and head back to the clubhouse. I need to contact Forest and see if we can get a trap set and catch Woolcombe before he hurts Pip.

To say I'm worried is an understatement as this bastard has murdered way too many so far. His links to the cartel are worrying me more than I am telling anyone.

Entering the clubhouse, I am meeting with the old boys, all four of them. They are standing with their arms crossed, looking to be updated with the latest.

"Come on, you four, let's go into Church where it's quiet," I tell them. I keep walking while I say that, too; I know they will follow.

Once they enter Church, I close the door, indicate they take a seat, and take my own. I look at each of them and then send a text with the picture of the box's contents and the note to each. I sit back with my arms crossed and wait for the fallout.

"What the fuck!" "Bastard," "Asshole," and "He's a dead man." are the comments I hear thrown out from them.

"We need to stop him. I'm going to speak to Forest about setting a trap. I tell them all. The last thing we need now is him taking us by surprise, we need to be the ones in charge, or Pip will pay the ultimate price, and I'm not willing to risk that."

"If any of you think of how we can trap him, bring it up in Church tomorrow. I am going to call the meeting later for early in the morning. We need to have an answer from Forest before that meeting, or I would call it today." I explain.

After we all throw a few ideas, we decide to think of ideas right up to tomorrow's meeting. I show them all out while they are still grumbling and cursing at each other and grab my cell to contact Forest.

I speak to Forest and update him on the latest event, and we talk a while discussing options of how we could catch this asshole. Eventually, Forest decides he will come to the clubhouse at the end of the week as he can't get away before that. He will bring a three-man team with him too.

I just have to keep Pip safe until then, and the weekend is the Thanksgiving dinner. I am sure she won't cancel that no matter what we all say to her.

****PIP****

After I get settled back in the apartment, I make a drink and sit in the lounge with Coal lying at my feet. I grab my cell and try contacting Liza again, still no answer. I ring the catering company's number once more, and someone answers.

After speaking to this woman, she informs me that Liza has not been at work for more than a week, and she has tried to contact her with no success.

Now I am worried, so I contact the local Police Department in Liza's hometown, see if they have any information at all, which they have not. I report her as a missing person, pushing that she has not been seen or heard from in over a week.

I get a list of hospitals for that area and start ringing one after another. Three down and nothing at all, but I am not going to let up now. I have three more to contact. I ring another and still nothing.

This one has an unidentified woman who matches Liza's description, but they tell me she had no identification and was severely beaten. They also told me she has lost her memory.

I ask if I text a photograph could they confirm or not if it is my best friend. I tell them she has no family, but we are like sisters, and that she was coming to me in Montana for Thanksgiving when her contract at her job finished.

Sending the photograph of myself and Liza to the number the woman gave me, all I can do now is wait while she checks out if it is Liza and gets permission to inform me once she knows. I will find out one way or another because I am happy to get a flight over to Nebraska if necessary.

Only twenty minutes later, the lady rings me back to inform me that it is Liza, but she has no memory of who she is. I give the woman all the details she will need and tell her I am her contact and that I will be there tomorrow.

I contact Brand and update him on what has happened and ask who can go with me tomorrow to Nebraska.

The following day sees Brand, Torch, Thunder, and myself at the airport. I have all the identification I will need to show I am the contact for Liza and that she will be coming home with us.

Arriving at the hospital, we are taken to a room, and the doctor meets with us. He lists all Liza's injuries, apart from the swelling on the brain she had, she also has a broken arm, three cracked ribs, multiple cuts, and black and blue everywhere.

To have this many injuries, she had to have been used as a punching bag. Tears are flowing down my face because this is my dearest friend, she is such a kind and good person, she would help anyone, and for someone to do this, they had to be evil.

I give all Liza's information and pay for her treatment as I don't have her insurance details, but I don't care either. I arrange for her to be ready to take with us to Montana, and he will update us on her follow-up appointments at our local hospital.

Now everything is settled, I can go and see Liza. Prepare her for the journey home and gently tell her who she is and what she is to me.

Torch has all the details of where she lives and will arrange to have her packed up and all forwarded to the clubhouse. Thunder is going with him to get her SUV as someone will have to drive her back as no way will she want to be seen on a flight looking beaten up.

We are taken to her room, and I stand outside the door and see her lying with a plaster cast on her arm. I hardly recognize her as her face is swollen and black, purple, and green. This is what she looks like, over a week after she was brought in. It is mind-numbing to think someone did this to her.

Just as I step into the room, Liza looks at me. I don't rush to her as I don't want to frighten her, but I calmly take hold of her hand when I reach the bed and gently smile at her with tears running down my face.

"Hi, it's me, Pip. I'm your sister, not by blood, but your sister just the same." I stand and wait and let her eyes rove my face.

"I don't know who you are," she responds, looking at me blankly, "Do you know my name?"

"Your name is Liza. Your full name is Elizabeth Michaels. You're a catering manager, and we went to catering school together. We both have our chef diplomas." I wait to see if she remembers anything now, I have given her this information.

"I don't remember."

"It doesn't matter, Liza. I have come to take you home with me. You were coming to me for Thanksgiving and then working with me until we have your own business up and running."

The nurse enters the room carrying a bag with medication inside. Pain medication and antibiotics as Liza will need to finish the course because of the cuts on her body. The pain medication she has to take every eight hours.

I get her dressed and signed out just as Torch and Thunder come back. Torch suggests that he and Thunder drive back to Nebraska with Liza as they can take turns driving, and that way, they won't have to do an overnight stay.

Liza seemed okay with that and said she would sleep all the way probably if she can lay down in the back because the pain medication knocks her out. So, we agree on that, and Brand and I fly back home.

****

Once home, I organize a room at the clubhouse for Liza as there is more help available here than if I put her in the apartment. The old boys are so good at getting people moving to get things done.

The new help is in place so on the whole things are running well. They all work rosters that keep everything running smoothly in the kitchen, and the meals are edible.

Sandy showed Mary everything she needed to be in charge and everything they had to know around the clubhouse.

Molly taught Frank all he needed behind the bar and stockroom. He seems excellent; he has an injury in his leg, but it doesn't seem to hold him up at all. He owned his own bar, so apart from working opposite Molly until new prospects are found, everything is working out ideal, and if needed, Thunder volunteered to do stand-in.

Crank has organized a nurse to come and change Liza's dressings every other day until she won't need them anymore. The last thing we want is for her to get an infection, although she is on antibiotics.

Thunder rang a while ago and gave us an estimate that they would be around another two hours but no more than that. He said she was doing okay, sleeping most of the way with the pain medication she's on.

While we are in wait mode, I decide to make some soup and rolls; then, if Liza doesn't want to eat much, it will be easier to get some of this down. She can't not eat when on the medication. We all need to be alert that she is having enough during the day.

Torch comes bustling through the door, and everyone wants to help any way they can. Some grab bags from the SUV, and Crank, of course, has to be involved by holding Liza's hand as though he is her dad. She keeps looking at him as though she is trying to remember him, which makes me smirk.

We get her settled in the room we set up, and I get some soup down her. She takes more pain medication and drops back to sleep.

I leave knowing she will be looked after as the old boys watch over her and spit orders whenever they think it is needed.

Torch shouts to me just as I call Coal to leave. Brand walks over as he is going with me, holding his hand out for the vehicle keys. Torch tells me that Liza will be okay. He will watch over her and for me to not worry as I have enough on my shoulders. I agree and tell him I will be back during the day tomorrow to have time with Liza as my being around may help her remember something.

He tells me not to try to rush her as it will come back when it is ready. He seems a bit overprotective, I think to myself. He is a great person, and if he is happy to look after Liza, then I won't stand in his way. He is tough, a bit rough on the edges, but one hell of a good man. What more could I want for my friend if that is where this is going.

CHAPTER 24

****BRAND****

Today, I hope we have some headway with the finding or trapping of Woolcombe. Forest is supposed to be here this morning sometime before lunch. I am having trouble keeping Pip from trying something she shouldn't, she is just strung up about Liza, and I don't think she is looking at the whole picture. But I am getting her concentrating on the Thanksgiving dinner tomorrow.

Pip's new staff are here helping her do all the prepping for tomorrow as she can't possibly do it all herself. There is a hell of a lot of us when you get us all in one place, and I smiled as she invited the new staff and their families. This woman is such a kind person; I don't think for a minute I deserve her, but I am not letting her go; I am going to be selfish and keep her.

I head out of the apartment and see Shoes just coming out of the trailer, so I wave him over.

"You're on duty here all day, and I want you to stay close to Pip," I state, giving him a stern look. "I've got this fucking feeling something is about to happen, but I can't put my finger on it."

"No problem, Pres, I will stay in the kitchen, or wherever Pip is, she won't like it, but what the hell, she will have to put up with it, I'll play the brother card." he snickers.

I hear a vehicle pull up and have to shake my head as Thunder and Crank turn up. They seem to have gone on guard duty without been called for it; they love my girl. I am happy to see it as she loves them back. I give them both a slap on their backs and make my way to my bike, telling them I will be back later in the afternoon.

Arriving back at the clubhouse, I see a vehicle I don't recognize. I point with a question to Billy 'The Kid', who is on gate duty. He shouts it is the Feds. I give him the thumbs up and make my way indoors.

Sniper and Glide are chatting with Forest and three others at the bar when I walk in. Making my way over to them, I point at the coffee machine to Molly, who is serving at the moment. She brings a tray over with cups and the coffee jug, so we all help ourselves.

Once we have our drinks, I indicate they follow me into my office. I don't want these fuckers in Church. They find themselves a seat, and I go and sit behind my desk.

"So, what have you come up with? Any ideas at all for catching this fucker?" I ask with a bit of snipe to my voice.

"We think the only way to catch him is to get Pip out in the open, but the trouble with that is it makes her vulnerable, especially if he has a sniper, and I won't put her at risk like that," he responds.

"We could put her in a vehicle and take her out to the food warehouse the next town over. It gets her away from here, and he would have to follow us to get any chance of getting near her." Thunder suggests.

"Risky, but we are running out of options. I think he is getting desperate." one of Forest's men says.

"I don't like that idea, it puts her out on her own, and I don't want to take that much of a risk." Brand responds, tapping his fingers on his desk.

"The Cartel in Mexico has been taken down. The only one who walked away was a nephew. He wanted to clean it up and take them out of the trafficking. He may keep it, but he is not as risky as the rest, and he wants to make the business legitimate, so the Mexican government has to make a choice, do they leave him and watch or just take him out too." Forest informs me.

"It is a damn messy business; they all deserve a bullet for what they have done to those innocent women." one of Forest's men comments.

"Back to the Pip business. What if we take her for a long walk in the back property? That could be somewhere he is hiding," Forest suggests. "If anything happens in there, it won't be witnessed either," he said with this look on his face that I don't even want to comment on.

"That is good, and she may go for that. She likes walking out there but hasn't because of this threat." I reply, twiddling my thumbs while I am thinking.

"Okay, let's just ask her what she thinks and go from there. What do you say?" Forest says as he is standing and stretching out.

Once we get to the restaurant, we go in through the front door, so Forest can see what we have achieved with this old building. He is impressed and commented how nice it looks, and the idea of day meals on the right and evening on the left was original, and he thought it would work well.

Pip comes out of the kitchen with Shoes just a few steps behind her, much to her disgust from the look she gives him. He, on the other hand, has a highly amused look spreading wider as I watch him.

"Hello Agent Forest, how are you?" she sweetly asks. God, I love this woman.

"I'm fine, Pip, thanks for asking," he responds and swipes his hand around to indicate the restaurant. "You have an amazing place here, it is stunning, and the layout is spot on. I wish you huge success with it."

She gives him her stunning smile, which I don't like. They should be just for me, I know it is irrational, but I don't care.

"Let me show you the kitchen and the apartment," Pip says as she is walking away.

We walk through the kitchen, and we dodge everyone working as we don't want to get in the way. Then she takes us out the back door and up the stairs to the apartment.

Once she opens the apartment door, Crank hugs her and excuses himself as he says he is going to stretch his legs. Coal, as always, is pleased to see her but keeps one eye on the men he doesn't know.

We wander through the apartment, and Forest makes all the right noises, which I have to say I appreciate as Pip has a beaming smile on her face.

I ask them all to take a seat in the lounge and update Pip on how to pull Woolcombe out so we can catch him. She is happy to go this afternoon either to the warehouse or out the back property. But not tomorrow as it is Thanksgiving.

It has to be today because tomorrow evening, Forest has to make his way back to Nebraska.

"Are you ready then Pip, we can go for a walk, and if you take your notepad, you can make out you're showing us where you are going to be building your house," I say. "It will give him the chance to come out."

"I'm not taking Coal as I don't want Woolcombe to have the option to hurt him," she states, and I understand that.

So, we all get ready to take a stroll. As we come back down the stairs, I note a black vehicle in the corner of the parking lot. I don't recognize it at all. Pip speaks to me, and it distracts me from where I was looking.

We go out the back, and Pip does an excellent job of trying to show us all the planning she has in mind, but I don't see anything out of the ordinary as I browse the surrounding area.

Walking even further onto the property, we are all on alert, but nothing seems to be out of the ordinary.

Making our way back to the parking lot, I get this feeling we are being watched. Under my breath, I say, "Think we're under observation, got a feeling."

"Yeah, I feel it too," Forest responds as he scans the area, trying not to be obvious about it.

As we step into the parking lot, the black vehicle is still there, and it is way off everything else, which makes it stand out pretty obviously. Something is not right. The hair on my neck stands up.

"Pip, get in the kitchen as fast as you can." I spit out and take my weapon out of my Kutte.

As Pip gets halfway toward the building, a scruffy man appears from the side of the building and points a gun at her.

Now everyone has a weapon out except for Pip. Who is frozen, not knowing if she should stand still or run for it.

"Are you an idiot, Woolcombe?" I shout, getting his attention away from Pip. "Do you see how many weapons are pointing at you! You have no chance of walking away from this alive if you fire your weapon."

"FBI stand down." one of Forest's men shouts.

"I'll shoot her," he stutters. "I have nothing to lose. I lost everything thanks to this bitch. All these years working to get what I want, and she ruins it in no time at all."

"No, you lost everything because you're an asshole," I shout to him, again getting his attention.

"You murdered my parents. You tried to murder me, and you deserve everything you get. You're an evil bastard who traffic's women to make a few dollars. I hope you rot in jail and become someone's bitch." Pip shouts at him.

If it weren't so serious, I would have laughed at her last comment, I didn't know she had it in her, but it is pretty damn arousing to hear.

"You won't get out of here alive Woolcombe put down your gun and hand yourself over to us," Forest states while taking a few steps nearer to him.

"I don't have to do fuck all. I'm the one who is walking away from this," Woolcombe shouts, he is getting more agitated, and I notice he is trying to step nearer to Pip.

"The cartel are all in prison or dead," Forest tells him, "Do you think you are going to make it out of this mess without any comeback at all. You're an intelligent man, so you have to know it cannot end well; it can't end with you getting anything you want."

I'm impressed with Forest as he is making steady headway toward this asshole without him realizing it. But I keep taking small steps toward Pip, who is still frozen to the spot.

"All your accounts are gone, all the money is with the FBI and being investigated, so we'll know what is legitimate money and what is from the shit you have been involved in," Forest's man tells him. "We have all the information you kept, so we know everything, literally everything you have been doing for the last 14 years."

All of a sudden, you can see he realizes he is in deep shit. He glances at his vehicle, and I know he is going to make a move for it. Without even thinking, I run for Pip and knock her down, covering her with my body because this asshole will not think twice about taking a pot shot as he runs for it.

At the same time, Woolcombe takes off for his vehicle, throwing himself into it. I look around and see the Feds still have their weapons trained on his car.

One of his men shouts to Forest should he take out his tires, but before he can answer, we hear the ignition click and BOOM! The vehicle explodes, and we're all flat on the ground covering our heads with our arms. I am still over the top of Pip, trying to keep her safe.

After a couple of minutes, we all stand up and look at the vehicle burning red. No way can we get him out. What's the point? The bastard's dead.

I look over at Forest, and he looks at me. We both shrug our shoulders, and I grab Pip into a hug.

The parking lot is full of people who have come outside to see what is happening, and Shoes rushes to us to make sure Pip is okay.

Forest tells us not to worry; he'll sort it all out, and nothing will come back on us, which I hope not as we had nothing to do with it, and the bastard deserved it.

When all the drama eases, we head indoors to the restaurant. We walk in, and the first thing I see is Crank, sitting with a cold one which he tips at me with a wink. I stand looking at him a minute as I don't understand why he has this look on his face, then it hits me, he was a bomb expert in the special forces. I give him my crooked smile and head nod and then burst out laughing. Of course, I don't tell anyone what I am laughing about, fuck that, I will keep this secret.

Forest's cell phone rings and he answers, walking away from everyone so no one can hear. A couple of minutes later, he walks over to Pip and asks if he can speak to her for a minute.

I keep my eye on them to make sure he doesn't upset her, and she looks okay when they walk back to me.

Pip tells me she has a few things to do in the trailer as her laptop is still there, so she potters off, shouting she will be back in a while.

****

Happy Thanksgiving, we all shout to each other and sit to enjoy a fantastic feast. We have love and laughter around us. Pretty damn amazing when you consider what we have all been through in the last months.

Pip is fussing over everyone, enjoying herself immensely. Shoes is having the first family Thanksgiving he has ever had and looks pretty smug with himself about it. Pip keeps calling him Bro' and smirking at him. She is up to something.

Pip leans over to Shoes and hands him an envelope, saying Happy Thanksgiving again. He hugs her and gives her a small parcel with fancy paper and a bow. She rips off the paper and opens the box.

Inside is a gold necklace with the word Sister and a diamond where the dot in the i of sister would be. Pip leans over and hugs Shoes tightly, and I see a tear sliding down her face. She kisses him on his cheek, much to his embarrassment, and makes him fasten it on her neck.

He opens the envelope and reads the paper inside. He looks at me as I know what it is, then he hugs Pip tightly. She just gave him a contract that is all paid for him to have his house built on the back property and 2 million in his bank account.

To my surprise, she hands me an envelope, which I open and find that Dollar has accepted 5 million into our club account, a gift that states it is to help anyone in the club that may need it.

Pip leans over and tells me that Forest had 10 million placed into her bank account, from the financials they found was legitimate from Woolcombe. All that money was from the business partnership, money he stole over the years.

Liza is very nervous but holding herself together. She is sitting with Torch and not letting him out of her sight. Pip gives her an envelope and once opened, it shows that Pip has given her friend 1 million.

Bill Forest and his team are at the table enjoying a meal with us. They are smiling and eating up a storm. They got rid of the vehicle and made sure we are all clear of any wrongdoing. Forest looks pretty smug as Pip is handing out her envelopes.

Spider is sitting with Jenna, his artist friend, now Pip's advertising manager. My woman seems to enchant everyone. Spider looks more than a little taken with his friend, I must admit.

Dagger is sitting with June, who is not shouting at him for once, and I thought I just saw a damn smile. Miracles happen. She is Pip's office manager, doing all the paperwork, ordering, etc.

The old boys are just enjoying everything by the looks of them. Thunder, as always, is laughing and joking around, Sniper is sitting with a smirk, Glide is taking it all in and storing anything he can use against the other three when he needs to, and Crank hasn't stopped with his little smile since yesterday, and I am not talking to him about it, ever.

But damn, I am thankful to him, and when I gave him a man hug last night at the clubhouse, he asked me if I'd grown a vagina, then mumbled *pussy whipped* under his breath, I was like, *what the fuck, man,* but laughed anyway.

Life is good, and I hope it stays this way for a long time.

BOOKS BY J.E DAELMAN

SATAN'S GUARDIANS MC

Book One - Brand

Book Two - Shades

Book Three - Odds

Book Four - Torch

Book Five - Ace

Book Six - Nash

Book Seven - Ink

Book Eight - Shadow

Book Nine - Christmas at the Clubhouse - Novella

Book Ten - Whisky

RAGING BARONS MC

Prequel - Truth and Lies

President - Axel - Book Two

Silver - Book Three

Fox – Book Four

Grease – Book Five

Hammer – Boos Six

BS – Book Seven

ACKNOWLEDGEMENTS

Firstly, thanks to Richard Tonge, who Alpha/Beta reads and Edits, you work so hard and I'm so grateful for all you do.

Thanks to my Alpha Reader on this book, Marie D Vayer [USA].

For my Beta readers, Karen Perez [USA], Sue Sumanski [USA], Vic Saunders [UK], and Emma Frost [UK].

My ARC team, you all keep me tapping the keyboard, giving me the confidence to carry on and enjoy my imagination. Thank you for each, and every review you write; every word means such a lot to me.

Lastly, thank you to my readers, who have reached out and given so many lovely comments about the books, especially your laughter about the old boys and their antics. I also thank you for the stunning reviews you place. Each one encourages a new reader to give the books a try ♥

~~*~*

YOU CAN FIND ME HERE:

Facebook Author page:
https://www.facebook.com/Jan.SGMC

Facebook Reader page:
https://www.facebook.com/groups/335434258378835

Twitter:
https://twitter.com/daelman_author

Instagram:
https://www.instagram.com/jandaelman_author/

MeWe:
https://mewe.com/i/jandaelman

Blog:
https://jdaelman-author.blogspot.com/

Goodreads:
https://www.goodreads.com/author/show/21391970.Jan_Daelman

BookBub:
https://www.bookbub.com/authors/j-e-daelman

SIGN UP FOR THE NEWSLETTER

https://www.subscribepage.com/u9r7b4

Printed in Great Britain
by Amazon